DANGEROUS DARK

Johnathan R Greene

Copyright © 2023 Johnathan Greene

All rights reserved

This is a work of fiction. names, characters, places, and incidents either are the product of the author's imagination or are used fictitiously. Any resemblance to actual persons, living or dead, events, or locales is entirely coincidental.

No part of this book may be reproduced, or stored in a retrieval system, or transmitted in any form or by any means, electronic, mechanical, photocopying, recording, or otherwise, without express written permission of the publisher.

ISBN-13: 9798398467994
ISBN-10: 1477123456

Library of Congress Control Number: 2018675309
Printed in the United States of America

CONTENTS

Title Page
Copyright
Epigraph
Introduction
Prologue
Chapter 1   1
Chapter 2   10
Chapter 3   16
Chapter 4   24
Chapter 5   30
Chapter 6   39
Chapter 7   45
Chapter 8   50
Chapter 9   57
Chapter 10   64
Chapter 11   71
Chapter 12   79
Chapter 13   89
Chapter 14   95
Chapter 15   103
Chapter 16   111

Chapter 17	120
Chapter 18	132
Chapter 19	137
Chapter 20	144
Chapter 21	153
About The Author	159

"Within the black canvas of the stars, our fates are painted."

UNKNOWN

INTRODUCTION

In a distant corner of the galaxy, an embattled group of Federation soldiers uncover a terrifying secret. Lead by the pragmatic Captain Reyes, these battle-hardened warriors find themselves faced with an insurmountable challenge. A city on the edge of nowhere, a crew lost in space, and a threat that could bring the Federation to its knees. Reyes and his team – the quick-witted Sergeant McKinley and the resourceful First Officer Moore – must navigate through danger, deception, and despair. Caught in a tangled web of power and betrayal, their resolve, loyalty, and courage are the only hope in a world on the brink of destruction. As the threads of fate weave a complex tapestry, the team finds themselves embroiled in a battle not just for their survival, but for the future of the Federation itself. Join them on their journey through uncharted territories, shadowy foes, and unexpected alliances. In this vast expanse, where hope seems scarce, they will discover that sometimes, the darkest moments give rise to the brightest stars.

PROLOGUE

In the year 2218 AD, an epochal shift marked human civilization. A super intelligent AI, Eidetic, ushered in a new era, propelling humanity into the golden age of space exploration. Guided by this AI, mankind discovered the Singularity Energy, which powers all facets of life including starships, with these starships humanity found a new frontier - the triple star system of Alpha Centauri. New settlements sprouted on celestial bodies, brightening the corners of the universe that had never seen life before. However, with new territories came new dangers, a lawless vastness that called for a protector. This guardian was Captain Eli Reyes, the seasoned commander of the "FSS Undaunting", an exploratory-class starship, under the direction of the United Federation of Sol Space Fleet. Reyes, once a starry-eyed boy enamored by the cosmic beyond, had now become a stalwart figure in the cosmos, a seasoned explorer turned defender. Captain Eli Reyes had a mission, one of immense responsibility and relentless vigilance. As the commander of the FSS Undaunting, his task was to safeguard humanity's interests in Alpha Centauri, to ensure that law and order prevailed amid the lawless expanse of the universe.

CHAPTER 1

Amid the undulating nebulae, the distant star clusters, and the cosmic ballet of Alpha Centauri, Captain Reyes found a strange, tranquil solace. His dark, watchful eyes, set beneath a furrowed brow, mirrored the depth and mystery of the universe he navigated. His seasoned face, marked by the scars of battles fought and won, was a testament to his survival instincts. Reyes was a tall, broad-shouldered figure with a commanding presence. His muscles, toned from years of military training and combat, rippled subtly beneath his uniform. His jet-black hair, streaked with traces of silver, was kept cropped short, adhering to the federation standards, while a short beard framed his strong, angular jawline. He moved with the stealthy grace of a seasoned warrior, his every gesture emanating a quiet strength and determination. Yet, his deep-set eyes bore a softness, a vulnerability that only those closest to him ever got to see. The vastness of the universe, rather than daunting, served as a constant reminder of the importance of his duty.
Captain Reyes was not just a soldier in the interstellar battlefield; he was a guardian of the fragile balance that held the universe together. Carrying this sense of purpose, he would retreat into his quarters, a sanctuary within the behemoth vessel, one wall entirely occupied by a floor-to-ceiling fish tank, where exotic, bioluminescent fish from across Earth's colonies

swam, casting a soft glow that reflected onto the polished steel surfaces. The room was otherwise dimly lit, but the stars outside bathed the quarters in a soft light that danced across the room, forming ever-changing patterns on the walls. Seated in a plush chair, engrossed in a holographic tablet.

The bright colors of the projection painted his face in an array of shifting lights as he flipped through the latest news from Earth and its sprawling colonies. The date was prominently displayed on the top corner of the tablet, ED, March 8th, 2318AD, a day just like any other, filled with promise and uncertainty. Scattered around the room were photographs, mostly of family, all frozen in moments of joy. Yet, one picture, however, stood out from the rest. It was a photograph of another soldier, clad in battle fatigues, a fellow officer in the military. The red background suggested it was taken on a Mars colony, a time and place etched vividly in Reyes' memory. The photograph acted as a portal, transporting Reyes back to a fierce battle on the Martian sands.

◆ ◆ ◆

Mars, 2298AD, a separatist group has rebelled against the federation, Reyes was tasked with leading a squad into battle and quell this rebellion. The red sands of Mars were kicked up into a crimson storm as laser fire zipped back and forth. Amidst the chaos, Reyes and this officer found themselves side by side, just as they had been many times before. Reyes, ever the optimist, had attempted to lighten the mood, "Just like the old days, huh Stevens?" His remark cut through the tension, a brief respite in the relentless storm of the battle. But, in the blink of an eye, the laughter was cut short. A laser blast had hit Stevens, its piercing red glow standing out starkly against the Martian landscape. In the aftermath, the battle had failed, and, in the confusion, Steven's condition was unknown. Despite extensive requests to the new Martian government, the United Federation of Sol never brokered a deal to recover Stevens' body.

◆ ◆ ◆

Brought back to the present, as his fingers lightly traced the edges of the holographic tablet, he said to himself "Lynn Stevens, damn good solider." as he continued to scroll through the news. The memory of Stevens and their shared battle, although painful, also steeled him further for the challenges that lay ahead. his eyes scanning but mind wandering, suddenly, the serenity of his quarters was shattered as his comms device crackled to life. First Officer Sarah Moore's voice came through, bringing him back from his thoughts, "Captain, Moore here. We have received a distress call from SS Serenity, a civilian transport ship, sir." Reyes set down his tablet, the holographic projections fading as his attention shifted to the task at hand. His gaze momentarily drifted to process her words, he spoke commandingly, "Roger, chart a course. Prepare the crew for a possible engagement, I'm heading to the bridge now, Reyes out." As the conversation ended, he stood, straightened his uniform, and gazed one last time at the distant stars. Then, with a deep breath, he stepped away from the viewport, readying himself to face whatever awaited him and his crew. "Let's do this." he said, the stars of Alpha Centauri as his backdrop, Reyes hastily left his quarters, his boots echoing down the metal corridors of the FSS Undaunting, each step resonating with a quiet yet unyielding determination. His crew, a collection of Earth's finest and bravest, saluted him as he passed, a silent testament to their unwavering trust in their captain. The bridge doors where now in sight, he paused for only a moment preparing himself, he entered, the doors hummed slightly as they slid open, revealing the bridge.

◆ ◆ ◆

The bridge of the FSS Undaunting bustled with a precise and quiet energy. A domed glass structure offering a breathtaking 360-degree view of the cosmic theater outside, the entire expanse of the triple star system of Alpha Centauri was on display. Embedded along the curvilinear walls, stations hummed with activity. Each was manned by a crew member, their fingers diligently working over consoles, their eyes focused on data streaming across screens. At the bridge's center, First Officer Moore commanded the helm. Moore, with her high cheekbones, sharp eyes, and short-cropped black hair, was a picture of focused intent.

Her orders flowed with practiced ease, guiding the crew with a calm certainty. "Raise the shields to maximum, prep the laser batteries, and alert medical for possible casualties," she instructed, her fingers nimbly manipulating the holographic control panel. Just as Moore was issuing her commands, the doors to the bridge slid open, and in strode Captain Eli Reyes. He moved with an effortless authority.

His eyes scanned the room, taking in the bustle of the bridge before finally resting on the large screen showing the SS Serenity's distress call. "Status report, Moore," he called out, his voice steady. "Sir, the SS Serenity sent out the distress call. They're reporting heavy damage and unknown casualties," Moore informed him, her voice carrying the grave implications of the situation. Reyes made his way to the Captain's Chair, a uniquely designed seat that hovered in the center of the bridge, the control hub of the mighty vessel.

As he settled into the chair, he intently studied the holographic screens depicting the damaged SS Serenity and a count of souls on board. "Any sign of the attackers?" Reyes questioned, his gaze narrowing on the fleeing blips on the screen. "Sir, there were three ships reported by the Serenity, which is confirmed by our scans. They're leaving the area," Moore relayed. A few moments of silence reigned as Reyes took in the information. Then, his decision came, firm and resolute. "Dispatch a rescue detachment to the Serenity immediately. As for those three ships, set us on a course to trail them, but keep our presence undetected. Engage silent running."

The FSS Undaunting sprang into action, each crew member executing their orders with skill and speed. Reyes remained in his Captain's Chair, his eyes holding the distant glimmers of Alpha Centauri, a steely resolve settling over him. As The Undaunting began to pivot, The Shadows of the Centauri were deep and dark, and he and his crew was ready to plunge into them, to ensure the safety of his people, outside the scene shifted. One of the Alpha Centauri stars was now behind the ship, casting long shadows over the panels and crew. The vessel slid stealthily through space, like a predator stalking its prey, undetectable against the cosmic backdrop.

The bridge, usually buzzing with energy, was nearly silent now. All attention was fixated on the task at hand, the usually humming consoles now reduced to whispers. The only sound was the soft hum of the ship's core, resonating like a quiet heartbeat through the silence. Captain Reyes sat in the heart of this silence, his eyes locked on the radar screen displaying the three triangle silhouettes representing the unknown ships. His fingers drummed lightly on the armrest of his chair, the only outward sign of his inner calculations. He motioned for Moore, who had been coordinating the rescue detachment for the SS Serenity, to come over. As she approached, he kept his gaze on the radar, the three silhouettes glowing ominously. "Moore," he began, his voice low but firm, "Once we get in close, identify these ships. Find out who our new 'friends' are, what their capabilities are, and most importantly, what their intentions might be." Moore nodded, her face set in a serious expression. She understood the gravity of the situation and the importance of this clandestine operation. "But" Reyes continued, his gaze finally shifting from the screen to meet Moore's, "we must not engage unless they fire on us first. If we maintain our silence, they might lead us to more answers. We're not just pursuing three rogue ships here; we're hunting for the truth." His words lingered in the tense air, a quiet resolve emanating from him.

As the Undaunting stealthily trailed the unknown ships, the vessel's advanced sensors began to pick up more detailed information. They were close enough now to discern more than just the ships' silhouettes. The sensor array began to identify telltale markers, indications that they were indeed dealing with pirate vessels. First Officer Moore analyzed the new data, her eyes darting over the stream of numbers and graphs. She relayed her findings to Captain Reyes. "Sir, the lead ship is showing unusual energy readings. It's nothing we've encountered before." Just as Moore was finishing her report, the ships on the radar abruptly changed course. They descended towards a moon orbiting a massive ringed gas giant that the Undaunting's star charts hadn't marked as a colonized location. Reyes eyed the change, his mind turning over the possibilities. "That moon isn't a known colony," he noted, "It could very well be a base of operations for these pirates." He was silent for a moment, considering their next move. "We need boots on the ground. Moore, you're with me. We'll need McKinley, too." Sergeant McKinley, a titan among the crew, was a veteran soldier, his tall and muscular frame covered in the scars of countless battles. His most distinguishing feature was the stark white blind eye, marked by a jagged scar that ran down his left cheek. When he stood, he towered over his fellow crew members, including the captain.

His voice, a gravelly baritone, echoed through the bridge as he acknowledged the orders. "Aye, with you captain" These three figures - Captain Reyes, First Officer Moore, and Sergeant McKinley - The moment had come to act, to leave the safety of their ship and venture into the unknown. They walked together towards the exit, their departure casting long shadows under the artificial lights of the bridge. The moment the door slid open, their conversation began, filling the quiet of the ship's sterile corridors.

Captain Reyes was the first to speak. "These energy signatures from the lead ship, they're puzzling. Any theories, Moore?" First Officer Moore, her mind already spinning with the puzzle presented, responded, "They're definitely not something we've seen before, Captain. It could be a weapon, a new propulsion system, or something else entirely. We won't know until we get a closer look." Just as Moore finished speaking, Sergeant McKinley's deep voice, carrying a thick Liverpudlian accent, broke through. "Aye, that we will. Not our first time dealing with unknowns, is it?" The captain glanced at McKinley, a small smile tugging at his lips, acknowledging the truth in his words.

They continued to stride down the long corridor, their footsteps echoing off the metal walls. Reyes spoke, his tone turning serious again. "That moon base, it isn't on any of our maps, which means these pirates either set it up recently, or they are damn good at hiding" Moore nodded, her eyes narrowing in thought. "That's concerning. It means we're walking into a potential trap. We need to be prepared for hostile forces, defenses, booby traps." Interrupting her in his gruff, gritty voice, McKinley added, "And don't forget, Captain, we're likely not to receive a warm welcome."

Finally, they arrived at the bay, bustling with activity, crew members swarmed around a sleek, black recon ship, carrying out final checks and pre-flight procedures. The sense of urgency was palpable, and yet each crew member moved with precision, aware that the mission's success heavily depended on their work.

First Officer Moore, with her signature meticulousness, personally inspected each part of the craft. She quizzed the engineers on their checks. "The thrusters, have they been inspected?" She asked. The chief engineer for the ship spoke in confidence. "Yes, ma'am, she's green across the board." Her sharp eyes missed no detail, her experience serving her well in moments like these. Suddenly, another figure rushed over to the group. Officer Albert Grant, a tall man with striking silver hair, a neatly trimmed beard and piercing blue eyes., late fifties, but his fit frame spoke volumes about his discipline and the hardy constitution of a veteran. He had an air of authority about him, a steadying presence on the ship, and was highly respected by his crewmates. Grant didn't waste any time on pleasantries, immediately launching into his strategic assessment. "This isn't a standard operation," he began, his voice steady and serious. "These aren't your typical pirates. They've set up base on an uncharted moon, evaded our patrols, and are potentially wielding unknown technology. Use extreme caution, and remember, our priority is to gather intelligence." His words, a blend of caution and motivation, hung in the air as the trio stood in silence for a moment, absorbing Grant's cautionary words.

The tension was high, but McKinley, the towering sergeant with the gritty Liverpudlian accent and a blind eye, was always good for some levity. "Unknown tech, yeah?" McKinley started, a smirk tugging at the corner of his mouth. "Last time I checked, they didn't make a blaster that could tickle me funny bone. So we're good there." As he began to laugh, he finished with, "I can do this all day." First Officer Moore rolled her eyes at McKinley's jest but couldn't help the smile that tugged at her lips. "That's what I'm afraid of!" she let out a chuckle as she continued "Me on the other hand" she paused turning to a more serious tone "I'm more concerned about the uncharted moon, we don't know what kind of environment we're walking into. Could be anything from hostile fauna to extreme weather conditions."

Captain Reyes nodded, a faint smile on his face as he took in their comments. "Right, and McKinley, keep that humor of yours at the ready. It might just very well come in handy. Let's remember what Grant said. Our priority is to gather intelligence. We move in, we gather what we can, and we get the hell out. No heroics." With a final nod of agreement, the three turned their attention back to the preparations, their banter cutting through the tension and serving as a reminder of the camaraderie and bond that had seen them through countless missions before. With their mission parameters established, the trio turned their attention to their gear. The Recon Suits they wore were a marvel of engineering: lightweight but strong, versatile yet intuitive. The helmet incorporated a Heads-Up Display that fed them critical information in real-time.

They each put one on, the suits seamlessly conforming to their bodies. "HUD check," Moore's voice came over the comms, her tone focused. The display in front of her eyes flared to life, status indicators lighting up green one by one. The suit was functioning as it should, and she gave a nod of satisfaction. The others followed suit, each confirming their systems were go. They moved next to the armory, selecting their weapons with practiced ease. Their choices reflected their roles and preferences - Reyes choosing a balanced plasma rifle, Moore picking up a sniper rifle with surgical precision, and McKinley selecting a heavy blaster that seemed a match for his towering frame. "Remember," Reyes reminded, as they secured their weapons, "we're there for recon, not to start a war." With their preparations complete, the trio made their way to the waiting recon ship.

The tension was thick as they climbed aboard, the hatch sealing behind them with a hiss. The launch bay was suddenly eerily silent, all eyes on the pod. "Undaunting, this is Recon One. We are green across the board. Ready for launch," Reyes reported. "Understood, Captain," came the reply from the control tower. "Godspeed." With a roar that was absorbed by the soundproofed bay, the recon ship detached, engines roaring to life, it's course, towards the unknown moon, carrying the trio into the uncertainty of Alpha Centauri, their mission, just beginning.

CHAPTER 2

Having arrived on the moon, the trio disembarked their ship, their boots crunching on the strange, silvery soil. It was a barren landscape stretched out before them, bathed in an ethereal light that was reflected off the gas giant this moon orbited. Craters and boulders dotted the horizon, providing the only variation in the monotonous panorama. Moore brought out her handheld scanner, its soft electronic hum barely audible over the low whistle of the wind. The device was state-of-the-art, capable of detecting life forms and technology over vast distances. Her brow furrowed as she checked the readings. "Sir, there appears to be nothing on my scanner," she reported. Reyes furrowed his brow in response, his eyes scanning the horizon. "That's strange indeed," he murmured. "We know for a fact we saw three ships on course, what are we missing?" That's when McKinley chimed in. His gruff voice carried a hint of humor as he said, "Maybe these blokes got they selves some invisibility cloaks, yeah? Guess they didn't get the memo" his voice lowering slightly "it's a bit out of fashion." Before anyone could respond to McKinley's joke, a faint thrum filled the air. The sound grew louder, transforming into the unmistakable roar of an engine. "Down!" Reyes ordered sharply, dropping to the moon's dusty surface. A ship, sleek and predatory, soared over their heads, close enough that the gust of its passing kicked up a veil of dust. It disappeared down a valley below, its noise slowly diminishing until the eerie silence returned. The team picked themselves up, dusting off their suits. Reyes gestured for everyone to follow him, his expression stern. "Let's see where our unexpected visitor is headed."

◆ ◆ ◆

The crest of the hill provided a sudden, sweeping vista that took their collective breath away. Nestled in the bowl of the valley, hidden from the prying eyes of space and any overhead scanners, was a massive city. Buildings of various sizes stretched out as far as the eye could see, illuminated by the cold, alien light of the moon. The city buzzed with activity - civilians hurriedly going about their daily lives, soldiers patrolling the streets, and towering cranes hinting at a city still expanding. At the far edge of the city, the ship they had seen earlier had landed on a designated pad. The whine of its engines was dying down, the glow of its thrusters cooling. Reyes pulled out a pair of binoculars, enhancing the visuals on his HUD. He focused on the landing pad, watching the ship's occupants disembark. They were clad in suits that hinted at a blend of human and alien technology and were met by a welcoming committee that was decidedly military. The exchange was brief, filled with salutes and gestures that spoke of a strict hierarchy. The group then disappeared from view, swallowed up by the city. Reyes lowered his binoculars, his expression thoughtful. The sight of an organized, bustling city on an uncharted moon was unexpected, to say the least. The presence of the military and their evident respect for the ship's passengers hinted at a complexity that went beyond mere piracy.

"I think we just found our pirates," he muttered, mostly to himself. "And it seems like they've made themselves quite at home."

"Scan shows it's teaming with life, sir," Moore reported. "That glow we saw from the ship in space? It's down there, somewhere under the city."

McKinley, leaning on his massive rifle, chimed in with a smirk. "Well, at least we won't be bored." He chuckled. "Seems like they've got themselves quite the right party down there." The team spent a while longer observing the city, taking in the patterns of life below them. They watched as patrols moved around the city, tracking their routines, their numbers. It was a puzzle that was slowly beginning to take shape in their minds. Reyes made the call, his voice grim. "Stow your weapons. We're going in, and we're blending in with the civilians." Moore looked at him in surprise, about to protest, but Reyes pointed towards a group of miners off to their right. They were heading back towards the city, their shift seemingly over, their clothing coated in lunar dust.

"No time for arguments. We're going in," Reyes said, already moving towards the group of miners.

The team fell in step behind him, stowing their weapons and adjusting their postures to resemble the weary, hunched miners. Seamlessly merging with the stream of weary miners, Reyes, Moore, and McKinley managed to blend in. Their faces smeared with artificial grime, they adopted the posture of workers drained from a day's labor. Their eyes focused on the ground, they trudged forward, ensuring they matched the sluggish pace of the miners.

As they approached the city's gates, their hearts pounded in their chests. Two burly guards, armed with menacing rifles, stood at the entrance. They eyed the incoming workers with a cold indifference, a clear sign of their desensitization to the daily grind. Suddenly, one of the guards jerked forward, the butt of his rifle striking a miner's kneecap with a sickening crunch. The miner collapsed with a whimper. The guard barked at him, "Get the lead out, keep moving!" The scene sent a ripple of unease through the group. Reyes, Moore, and McKinley steeled themselves, carefully avoiding the guard's gaze. They continued to shuffle forward, the city's gate now looming large in front of them. With their hearts in their throats, they made it through the entrance.

Once safely inside the city, the trio subtly broke away from the stream of miners and resumed a more natural pace. The city unfolded around them in a tapestry of grim scenes. There were no smiling faces here, no laughter or easy banter. Only a sea of tired eyes and weary souls, weighed down by the harsh realities of their existence. Armed patrols marched through the city streets, their armored suits clanking in unison. The faceplates of their helmets were down, rendering them faceless, inhuman. A shiver of unease ran down their spines at the sight. This wasn't a city. It was a labor camp, a prison in all but name. Moore voiced what they were all thinking. "These people... They're not here by choice," she murmured, her gaze scanning the downtrodden faces around them.

"They're being forced to live and work here." Reyes nodded, his jaw clenching. He felt a surge of anger, an urgency. This wasn't just about securing the technology anymore. It was about liberating these people from their captors. "We need to end this," he said, his voice firm. "And we need to do it soon." Even McKinley, who was always ready with a quip or a wisecrack, had a grim expression on his face. "This isn't right," he grumbled, his usually vibrant voice subdued. "People shouldn't have to live like this." Reyes, Moore, and McKinley pushed on, their goal the large structure where the ship had landed. Reyes pointed towards it, determination in his eyes. "Wherever that group went," he said, "they're the key to all this. They're running this place. We find them, we find our answers." With this new resolve, they navigated the sprawling city.

The armored patrols were a constant threat, their intimidating presence making the journey even more treacherous. Using their tactical training, they stealthily evaded the patrols, slipping into narrow alleys and hiding in shadows whenever necessary. Despite the risks, they moved with purpose, always mindful of their objective.

◆ ◆ ◆

Upon reaching their destination, the trio was faced with a heavily fortified entrance teeming with guards. McKinley chuckled, shaking his head. "Well, that's one way I definitely wouldn't recommend." They looked around, weighing their options. Moore was tapping away on her device, her brows furrowed in concentration. After a moment, she looked up, gesturing towards a manhole cover a short distance away. "The city's underground sewer system," she said. "It might be our best bet."

Reyes nodded, his gaze sharp. "Let's move," he ordered. Quickly yet cautiously, they made their way to the manhole cover. After ensuring the coast was clear, they quietly pried the cover off. One by one, they descended into the darkness below, their figures swallowed by the shadows. McKinley, the last to enter, carefully slid the cover back into place with a faint thud. The streets were quiet once more, the trio's presence reduced to a mere whisper in the city's underbelly.

Tucked away within bowels of the city, the trio activated lights mounted on their forearms. The faint glow pierced the murky darkness, revealing the dank and grimy surroundings. Pipes of all sizes crisscrossed overhead, and the sound of rushing water reverberated through the tunnel. Moore had her face close to her scanner, the soft blue light from its screen casting an ethereal glow on her features. "This way," she murmured, navigating through the labyrinthine network of tunnels that sprawled before them. McKinley, unaccustomed to the stifling stench that permeated the air, wrinkled his nose. He couldn't help but make a quip, despite their tense situation. "Fuckin 'ell! This reminds me of the time I got stuck in a waste processing unit on Ganymede," he exclaimed in his Liverpudlian accent, with an irreverent grin. "Makes me almost miss that place! Almost."

Reyes shot a glance back at McKinley, an amused glint in his eyes contrasting with his stern demeanor. "McKinley," he said, his voice echoing slightly in the cavernous sewer, "pipe down!" The smile that curled at the edges of his lips belied the severity of his words. "We definitely don't need our 'friends' up there to know we're right under their feet." With that they pressed onward, the light from their forearm lamps dancing off the grimy walls.

The sense of urgency fueled their steps, as they ventured deeper into the underbelly of the mysterious city. Navigating the serpentine tunnels, they were nearing their destination. Moore's handheld scanner pinged softly, indicating the close proximity of the energy source they had been trailing. Ahead, an iron grate partially obscured their view of a large, open chamber. Soft, unnatural light emanated from within, its source: a large, cylindrical object suspended mid-air, pulsating with an unknown energy. Its glow painted eerie shadows on the surrounding walls, lending a sinister quality to the chamber. Footsteps echoed through the chamber, drawing their attention. A figure detached itself from the shadows, entering the lit area. This figure was taller and bulkier than the others they had seen, clad in heavier armor. The figure paused, scanning the room before proceeding towards the pulsating energy source. Reyes, Moore, and McKinley hunkered down behind the grate, their breaths held, as they observed the figure's movements.

CHAPTER 3

The imposing figure now standing near the glowing energy source, as it was lowered to the floor. Another, smaller figure followed him.
"All is ready, sir," the second figure spoke, his voice echoing slightly in the cavernous room. "We can commence whenever you command."
The lead figure chuckled, a low, rumbling sound that echoed ominously throughout the chamber. "Excellent," he responded, his voice thick with satisfaction. "With this device, I can bring the Federation to its..." He paused, his gloved hand caressing the device as he lingered over his words, "...knees."
From their hidden vantage point behind the grate, Reyes, Moore, and McKinley exchanged worried glances. "That's not good," Moore whispered, her voice barely audible over the hum of the device. "We need to find out what those plans are." With that, they fell back into silence, watching and waiting, as they tried to gather more information on the imminent threat facing the Federation. They knew they were in deep, but the stakes had just risen higher than they could have imagined. As the lead figure continued his inspection, he turned towards the hidden observers, his face finally revealed in the glow of the strange device. It was a face Captain Reyes hadn't seen for many years, one he had believed lost forever. It was the face of Lynn Stevens. Shock, disbelief, and a surge of myriad emotions paralyzed Reyes. Moore and McKinley noticed their leader's sudden

change. "Captain?" Moore asked, her voice filled with concern. No response.

"Cap?" McKinley tried again, his usual jokes set aside in light of Reyes' reaction. Reyes remained silent, his gaze fixed on the figure who was supposed to be his long-lost friend.

"Reyes, what's wrong?" Moore asked, her voice barely above a whisper, her eyes darting between their captain and the figure in the room beyond. It took another moment before Reyes finally found his voice, his eyes never leaving the figure of Stevens.

"That's... That's Lynn Stevens," he murmured, his voice strained with disbelief. The revelation hung in the air between them, heavy and ominous as they grappled with this unexpected twist. "Lynn Stevens sir? who might that lad be?" McKinley said. "Lynn...Lynn is... was a comrade. We attended the academy together. Both assigned to the same platoon when war broke out with the separatist group on Mars," Reyes began, his voice distant as he recalled the past. "We were squad leaders but, in one particular battle, our units ended up together. That's... that's the last time I saw him." Reyes paused for a moment, gathering his thoughts. "During that chaotic battle, he was hit by a laser blast," he continued, his voice growing heavy. "We lost that war and in the confusion that ensued. the Federation couldn't recover his body. We... we all presumed he had been killed in action." Reyes let out a long sigh, his eyes never leaving the figure of Stevens. "To see him here, seemingly leading this operation... it's... it's unthinkable," he murmured, the shock evident in his voice.

Moore and McKinley exchanged worried glances, the burly Sergeant's words echoed the thoughts of the group, his heavy Liverpudlian accent breaking the heavy silence that had fallen. "Bloody 'ell, boss," he repeated, shaking his head slightly, his gaze fixed on the scene unfolding beyond the grate. "That's not good at all."

The implications of their discovery were massive. Not only was their mission now significantly more complicated, but it also carried a weight that was deeply personal. As they continued to observe, each lost in their thoughts, a new determination settled within them. They have to figure out what Stevens is up to, stop whatever plans he has set in motion, and if possible, bring Stevens to justice. A moment of silence echoed in the grimy confines of the sewer. Reyes' heart pounded like a war drum in his chest as he watched the figure of Lynn Stevens, an apparition from his past, casually strolling around the mysterious object. Suddenly, the silence was broken by the quiet chirp of his communication device. It was the Undaunting.

"Captain Reyes, we have multiple unknown signatures on an intercept course," reported the voice of the Undaunting's AI. It was a calm, contrastingly at odds with the imminent danger it was reporting.

Reyes' hand clenched tightly around the device. "Impossible," he shot back, his eyes still fixated on Stevens. "You're running silent, they shouldn't be able to see you." "Well, sir," came the undeterred AI response, "they are on an intercept course. We're detecting multiple laser batteries coming online."

The news hit Reyes like a punch to the gut. Above them, the Undaunting was being surrounded, caught off guard, while they were meters below the surface, trapped in a labyrinth of sewers. They were cornered, and time was running out.

"Engagement initiated, sir. We're taking evasive action," the AI reported, a flicker of urgency now creeping into its usually calm voice. The line went silent, leaving the chilling sound of combat echoing in the distant space. Back through the grate, the view of the facility shifted. A guard hurried towards Stevens, whispered something into his ear. The relaxed, confident demeanor on Stevens' face hardened almost immediately. His orders echoed through the large space, reaching Reyes and his crew through the grate.

"Lock down the city. High alert! No one gets in or out without my approval!" His voice, authoritative and cold, sent a chill down Reyes' spine. Stevens then disappeared down a nearby corridor, leaving the crew in the now buzzing facility. The city above would soon be in a lockdown, the facility they were in, a fort.

Their predicament had just become a whole lot worse.

"Sir, we're taking heavy fire... Shields at 20% and falling..." The voice from the Undaunting crackled through the comms, background noise filled with the cacophony of alarms and orders being barked. "I'm ordering ship abandonment, sir. We've taking heav..."

The line went dead. Silence engulfed the sewer, save for the distant hum of the city and the echoing words of the Undaunting. Reyes quickly attempted to reestablish the connection, fingers flying across his wrist device. But there was nothing, only an ominous silence that screamed louder than any battle cry.

"We have to get out of here," Reyes voiced out, his face a grim mask. His gaze met Moore and McKinley's, both mirroring the same determined resolve. They were alone now, their ship and crew - potentially gone. The reality of their situation was closing in, but there was no time to mourn. They had a mission to finish, and a planet to save. As they made their exit from the grate viewing area, they plunged back into the dismal maze of the sewer tunnels, their steps urgent and hurried. The sickening stench that McKinley had jokingly referenced earlier was now a stark reminder of the harsh reality of their predicament. Moore was quick to redirect their course, her scanner's readings guiding them through the labyrinthine underbelly of the city. "This way," she prompted, gesturing towards a tunnel veering sharply to the right. The captain and the towering sergeant followed suit without hesitation, their previous course abandoned instantaneously. The sound of their boots splashing against the grimy sewer water was a constant, dissonant symphony in the background, echoing off the dank and mold-ridden tunnel walls. Every scurry of a rat, every drip of water leaking from the aged pipelines above punctuated the urgency of their situation. With the hostile city looming just above them, they navigated through the darkened tunnels, each step taking them further away from the grim cityscape, yet closer to an uncertain future. The only thought in their minds was survival and getting word to the Federation about the impending danger. They had no idea what lay ahead, but surrender was not in their vocabulary. Inching their way through the dark, the sliver of natural light at the end of the tunnel seemed like a beacon of hope amidst the darkness. The dreadful stench of the sewers started to wane and was slowly replaced by the raw scent of the moon's dirt and rock.

Moore, still leading the pack, pointed at the light source, her voice echoing through the tunnel, "We're almost there, this is our way out!" The rest of the team, driven by the prospect of escape, quickened their pace. McKinley, despite his massive frame, moved swiftly, his boots splashing rhythmically in the shallow waters of the tunnel. Reyes followed suit, the glimmering light source providing a renewed surge of energy. Sweat dripped down their faces, the reality of their predicament driving them forward. The closer they got, the stronger the light became.

As they neared the exit, they could begin to make out the details of the outside world. The barren, rugged landscape of the moon lay sprawled out in front of them. But the relief of escape was quickly replaced with the challenge of surviving in the open wilderness of the moon's surface. They were out of the city, but their mission was far from over. Emerging from the confines of the sewer system, they were met with the stark, desolate beauty of the moon's surface. The crater-riddled landscape stretched out before them, providing a stark contrast to the bustling activity they'd left behind in the city. The sky above was a breathtaking canvas of twinkling stars and galaxies, painting a vivid picture of the infinite expanse of space. Reyes, taking in the sight, turned to face his team. His voice came out as a grim determination in their earpieces, "We need to find our ship, it's equipped with a distress beacon. We activate it, then... we wait and hope that the Federation is able to pick up our signal." The gravity of the situation was not lost on them, yet there was an unwavering resolve in their faces. They had survived so far, they were not about to give up now. With a curt nod, Moore and McKinley acknowledged their orders. The trio began their journey across the moon's desolate landscape, their survival instincts kicking in as they moved towards the location of their ship. Their journey was marked by the stark silence of the moon, broken only by the crunch of their boots against the lunar regolith.

Each step they took was a testament to their determination to survive, their resilience shining through even in the face of an uncertain future. The landscape of the moon, while barren and desolate, provided ample opportunities for cover. Low, craggy hills and deep, shadowy craters concealed their movement, turning their journey into a silent game of hide-and-seek with the patrolling ships. Each shift in the shadows, every ripple in the air, made them hold their breath, their hearts pounding in their chests. A particular heart-stopping moment arrived when a patrol ship flew dangerously close. Its bright searchlights swept across their path, its droning engines growing louder with each passing second.

McKinley, who was leading at that moment, spotted a nearby cave. With a swift hand signal, he motioned for the team to dive into it. They scrambled into the safety of the cave, their breaths coming out in ragged huffs as they pressed themselves against the cold, rough walls. The entrance of the cave was bathed in blinding light as the ship passed by, its engines reverberating against the cave walls. They could see the ship's underside as it passed overhead, the ominous hum of its engines filling the silence around them. It was an agonizing moment, their lives hanging in the balance. They held their breaths, praying the ship would move on. After what felt like an eternity, the light began to fade, the roar of the engines diminishing as the ship moved away. Once the sound had fully receded, they allowed themselves a moment to exhale, their breaths coming out in shaky bursts. That had been too close. But they had made it, undetected. They exchanged brief, grim nods, acknowledging their narrow escape before stepping back into the lunar landscape, continuing their silent trek towards their ship.

◆ ◆ ◆

In the harsh emptiness of the lunar horizon, the trio watched with heavy hearts as a streak of fiery debris clawed its way across the sky. It was the Undaunting, their beacon of hope, now a flaming specter succumbing to the merciless gravity of the moon. The vessel's deorbiting plunge was a gut-wrenching spectacle, its once gleaming hull now ablaze, churning smoke and fire in its wake. The Undaunting's fiery descent ended in a thunderous crash that shook the lunar surface, the shockwave visible even from their distance. A plume of dust and debris bloomed into the airless sky, a silent testament to the violence of its impact. The sight was a devastating blow, the loss of their vessel - their home and symbol of security - was a heavy burden to bear. But amidst the sorrow and disbelief, there was an undeniable opportunity before them.

The city was thrown into a frenzy, the populace and patrols distracted by the spectacle and scrambling towards the crash site. Vehicles and ships broke away, racing towards the wreckage like scavengers to a feast. A solemn silence hung between the three of them, the weight of their loss heavy in the air. Yet, their mission wasn't over. Their heads hung low, more in determination than defeat. Captain Reyes, the grief evident in his voice, said, "We need to keep moving. We still have a chance to send that distress signal." Their grim determination rekindled, they pressed on.

With every step towards their hidden ship, they moved further from the chaos of the city and closer to achieving their mission. The odds were against them, yet they held onto the hope of sending that distress signal. They couldn't fail now. Not while the memory of the Undaunting was still fresh in their hearts. With a renewed sense of urgency, the trio trudged across the vast, desolate landscape, weaving their way through jagged lunar craters and steep ridges. In the distance, the gleaming silhouette of their hidden ship, an oasis amidst the desolation, finally emerged.

The sight of it ignited a sliver of hope amidst their dire situation. Captain Reyes was the first to reach the ship, his gloved hand running over the cold, metallic hull with a touch of relief. McKinley and Moore soon joined him, their ragged breaths echoing inside their helmets. They had made it. Quickly, they clambered aboard, their heavy boots echoing in the narrow confines of the ship. Moore immediately set to work on the communications array, her fingers dancing over the controls as she sent their distress signal, broadcasting their desperate plea into the void. Minutes felt like hours in the tension-filled silence as they waited for a response.

Finally, the communication console crackled to life. A voice cut through the static, an anchor in the sea of their despair. It was the Federation. "This is the Federation Star Command, we've received your distress signal. Hold tight, Undaunting. Rescue is one day out." Relief washed over the three of them, the tension in the ship lessening at the promise of rescue. They had survived, they had succeeded in their mission, and now, they had hope. They exchanged weary but determined looks. Their ordeal was not over yet, but they knew they would not face it alone, the battered but unbroken trio settled into their ship, the beacon of their distress signal glowing against the moon's desolate landscape, their eyes firmly set on the star-studded horizon. Tomorrow, the Federation would arrive, and with it, their salvation.

CHAPTER 4

The dawn of the next day saw the trio in a state of uneasy rest within the confines of their ship. The tension was palpable, each passing second felt like an eternity as they waited for their rescuers from the Federation. Yet, the silence of their wait was abruptly broken by a crunching sound. Through a small porthole, Captain Reyes saw a squad of heavily armed figures approaching their ship. The harsh lunar light glinted off their armor, their formation and movement screaming 'battle-ready'. The leader, an imposing figure even from afar, signaled his men to spread out, his orders cutting through the still lunar air. Reyes' heart pounded in his chest. "We've got company," he rasped, alerting Moore and McKinley. The once quiet ship was now a hive of activity. The trio moved with a practiced efficiency, slipping into their respective roles with grim determination. This was a scenario they had trained for, prepared for, yet hoped would never come.

Moore took up a defensive position by the entrance, her weapon primed and ready. McKinley moved to cover the rear, his eyes scanning the moon's surface for any signs of flanking.

Reyes took the lead, his pulse rifle steady in his grip. The crunching sound grew louder, the shadows of the approaching squad growing longer as they neared the ship. "Ready," Reyes whispered, his voice steady despite the pounding of his heart. Their wait was over. The battle was about to begin. With that,

Reyes' slammed his fist onto a button nestled within the main console, the exterior doors of their ship flung open abruptly. The sudden movement took the approaching squad by surprise, and they immediately turned their attention towards the now exposed entrance.
Their leader, thrown off for a moment, threw up an arm signaling his group to halt. An uncertain silence hung in the lunar air. Suddenly, the tranquility shattered. The trio burst forth from the open doors, their weapons blazing with hot laser fire. The ensuing battle was short but intense, and the once threatening squad was dispatched with well-rehearsed precision.
As the final enemy fell, an unexpected sound filled the air - the deafening boom of space-time rupturing. Reyes, Moore, and McKinley all turned their gaze skyward, witnessing a fleet of starships materializing into existence, each emerging from a point of warped space. Reyes' communicator crackled to life, a calm voice assuring, "Captain, this is the FSS Independence, heard you folks needed a rescue."
Yet, as he looked back, Reyes spotted a group of transport ships darting away from the moon in haste. He squinted, recognizing the formation, "That has to be Stevens." He muttered to Moore and McKinley. From their vantage point, they could see Federation troop transports descending upon the beleaguered city. The orderly procession of the landing crafts was punctuated by flashes of conflict, skirmishes breaking out as the Federation forces clashed with the remaining hostile elements.

◆ ◆ ◆

Rescue finally arrived for Reyes' team in the form of a swift, armored recovery shuttle. As the shuttle's doors slid closed, the lunar city was a receding panorama of smoke and swirling lunar dust. Just as suddenly as the chaos had unfolded, it was replaced by the serene blackness of space.
The starlight painted an almost tranquil picture, their escape

a stark contrast to the turmoil they had just left behind. The liberated city below was now in the hands of the Federation, their mission complete. But with Lynn Stevens still at large, they knew their battle was far from over. The rescue shuttle had whisked them away from the war-torn surface of the moon, they had their first glimpse of the grand vessel that would serve as their new temporary home. The shuttle's trajectory took them gliding across the colossal hull of the starship, its name etched proudly against the sheen of the cold metal: FSS Independence.

The silence within the shuttle was finally broken by McKinley. With his characteristic Liverpudlian accent, he quipped, "Well ain't that a right knee-slapper? A Yank and a Brit hitching a ride on the 'Independence'. Bloody 'ell, you lot sure know how to rub it in, don't you Captain?" The rest of the shuttle erupted into much-needed laughter, the tension of the past day's events momentarily forgotten, still chuckling, Moore turned to McKinley, her eyebrows raised in curiosity, "Alright, McKinley, we've known each other for what, a couple of years now? And I just realized I don't know your full name."

McKinley shot her a cheeky grin, "Oh, look at you getting all sentimental on me, Moore." Moore simply crossed her arms and returned his grin with a challenging smirk. McKinley sighed, rolling his eyes theatrically before letting out a soft laugh. "Alright, alright. Name's Harry McKinley. Harry after my grandad, and McKinley... well, you already know that bit. My mum was dead set on it, even if it gave me dad a bit of a worry, thinking I'd be too posh for our humble Liverpudlian roots."

His words hung in the air for a moment, filling the shuttle with an endearing warmth as they continued their journey towards the FSS Independence.

❖ ❖ ❖

Now aboard the Independence, they were greeted by its commanding officer, a stern-faced woman with silver hair and sharp eyes that spoke of years in service.

Captain Claudia Avery stood tall and saluted them, "Captain Reyes, it's a pleasure to meet you in person." Before Reyes could return her greeting, the Captain's communication device blared with an urgent update, "Captain Avery, the city has been secured. However, the base Reyes described is empty." Avery relayed the message back to Reyes, her brows furrowing in concern. Reyes sighed deeply, his gut confirming what he already suspected, "I had a feeling Stevens would make his escape with the device." Avery gave Reyes a serious look, "That's not just any device, Reyes. It's a weapon – Federation technology.

It was designed to blast away huge mountain ranges for our colonization efforts. If Stevens has it, there's no doubt he intends to use it." "But on what?" The question hung heavily in the air as they all mulled over the dire implications.

The thought of a weapon of such magnitude in the hands of a renegade like Stevens was a nightmare they were now forced to confront. "Captain Avery," Moore interjected, her brow furrowed in concern. "Before the attack, Stevens said something... about bringing the Federation to its knees." Avery looked at Moore, then back to Reyes, her expression grave. "We'll have to consider every word, every action. For now, though, we need to get you all back to Earth. Fleet Command will want a full report, Captain Reyes."

She then turned away, speaking into her communication device. "First Officer, chart a course for Earth, maximum warp. We've got important cargo to deliver." The reality of their situation was finally settling in. A rogue officer, a powerful weapon, a dire threat - the weight of it all rested heavily on their shoulders as the Independence prepared to warp towards Earth.

With the command given, the ship started humming as it prepared to leap into warp. McKinley, ever the child at heart, quickly made his way to the nearest viewpoint, his eyes lighting up with excitement. "I'll never get tired of this!" he shouted over the low hum of the warp engines. His wide grin was infectious, a moment of levity amidst the tension. He pressed his face against the glass, watching as the stars stretched into streaks of light. The swirling colors of the warp tunnel engulfed the ship, making it seem as if they were shooting through a kaleidoscope of cosmic hues. The intense feeling of speed was deceptive, almost surreal. To think they were crossing distances that would take generations to traverse at the speed of light. It was a spectacle that never lost its thrill, no matter how many times you experienced it. "Follow me to the bridge, please," Avery commanded as she led the group with McKinley playing catch up. As they moved through the labyrinthine corridors of the Independence, they exchanged brief words, discussing the mission and their next steps.

"So, what happened out there? In more detail," she prodded, casting a glance over her shoulder at Reyes. Reyes took a deep breath, recounting their journey through the pirate base, the discovery of the massive weapon, and their harrowing escape. Avery with concern interjected, "From your description, it sounds like Stevens is planning something big," Moore, her gaze serious spoke, "Ma'am, we are dealing with a highly intelligent, highly motivated enemy here. Stevens isn't just a rogue officer - he's a threat to the Federation. He has access to our technology, our intel. He's dangerous." The corridors seemed to stretch on indefinitely, a testament to the scale of the starship. Finally, they reached a door, which slid open with a soft hiss, revealing a large room filled with blinking consoles and uniformed officers. It was the bridge of the Independence. As they stepped onto the bridge, the timing couldn't have been more perfect.

The swirling colors of the warp tunnel subsided as they dropped out of warp. The view ahead was suddenly filled with the blue-and-green marble of Earth. It seemed to grow in size rapidly as the ship continued its approach, a stunning spectacle of oceans, clouds, and continents. Their casual chatter subsided, each crew member pausing to take in the sight of their home planet, a stark reminder of what they were fighting for. Even McKinley, always ready with a joke, was quieted by the view.

As they neared Earth, it was clear their mission was far from over. The Earth continued to grow in size through the bridge's viewport, the trio began to give their goodbyes to the crew of the Independence. Handshakes, nods, and words of gratitude were exchanged, along with a few solemn smiles. Reyes, taking the lead, thanked Captain Avery for her assistance and leadership. "You run a tight ship, Captain Avery," he commented, offering her a salute of respect. She returned it with a smile, "Just doing my duty, Captain Reyes. Safe travels." Moore and McKinley followed suit, bidding the crew farewell before they exited the bridge. As they journeyed through the corridors towards the ship's airlock, they were met with nods of respect and well-wishes from the ship's crew.

A transport ship had docked, ready to ferry them down to Earth. Stepping inside the transport, they strapped themselves into the seats, a sense of anticipation filling the air. The transport disengaged from the Independence and began its descent, they could see the blue-green sphere of Earth growing larger. And thus ended their time on the Independence. As the Earth filled their view, they knew their fight was not over. Their adventure, though fraught with danger and uncertainty, was just beginning.

CHAPTER 5

The Earth shimmered like a precious blue gem as the transport ship descended from the inky blackness of space. The trio gazed down in awe at the sight below. The city of New York was a pulsating mass of light and life, a tapestry of glass, steel, and verdant greenery that sprawled across the landscape. Skyscrapers kissed the sky, their sleek, eco-futuristic designs standing testament to human ingenuity. Wind turbines and solar panels studded the rooftops, while vertical gardens clung to the buildings, infusing the concrete jungle with streaks of green. As the shuttle skirted the glowing boundaries of New York, Reyes, looking at the city sprawling below, began to speak, his voice filled with a deep nostalgia. "Ah, New York, the city of dreams," he began, "dreams of ambitions, of hope and despair, of growth and transformation." He gestured towards the eco-futuristic skyline, his eyes following the lines of the skyscrapers stretching into the clouds. "Once, it was a city of steel and smoke, filled with the constant noise of machines and people alike. It was the bustling heart of a burgeoning civilization, throbbing with energy, ceaselessly marching towards the future." "But as humanity spread its wings into the vast cosmos, our home too began to transform." His hand swept across the landscape, tracing the green veins of gardens that hugged the buildings and the wind turbines dotting the horizon. "From the ashes of the old world, New York rebirthed itself into the eco-conscious marvel you see today. Today, it stands as a testament to the resilience of humanity, to our ability to evolve and grow." As Reyes spun his tale, McKinley and Moore listened, their expressions rapt. McKinley, a slight twinkle in his eyes, spoke up first. "Y'know, being starborn, Earth was like a fairy tale to me. Just stories woven from starlight and void. Tales of a 'blue marble' with open skies, wild oceans, and green lands," he glanced out at the city once again. "Seeing it now, it's like walking into that fairy tale," he chuckled, "Only difference, I expected more dragons." The trio shared a laugh, the tension from their mission momentarily forgotten. As the laughter subsided, Moore added, "I was born on Europa. I grew up watching Jupiter rise over the ice fields, its bands of color always dancing across the sky. But Earth..." she paused, "Earth was something different. A planet teeming with life, with history. I always dreamed of seeing it. And now here we are, descending into the heart of it." Their shuttle ride became a journey through stories and shared dreams, their personal tales merging with the grand tale of humanity's growth and evolution. The city beneath them, bathed in the soft glow of the setting sun, seemed to welcome them home, a beacon of hope and resilience in a vast universe. Their shuttle landed gently on the landing pad of the Federation's headquarters. The building towered above everything else, its height only matched by its architectural beauty. It was an edifice of shimmering glass, reflecting the sunlight in a thousand different hues, ensconced in a lush green expanse that seemed to breathe with life. A representative of Federation Command, a woman in her mid-thirties with a stern gaze and a sleek, military-style bun, awaited them on the landing pad. Dressed in the immaculate dark blues of the Federation's uniform, highlighted with hints of gold insignia, she saluted them crisply. "Captain Reyes, Lieutenant Moore, and Chief Engineer McKinley, I presume?" she asked, her voice firm yet welcoming. "I'm Lieutenant Commander Jenkins. Welcome to Federation Command." After brief introductions and handshakes, she motioned for them to follow her, "Command has been expecting you. They're eager to debrief on your recent encounter." As they strode through the halls of the headquarters, the trio couldn't help but marvel at the striking blend of tradition and innovation. Along the halls, artifacts from human history were interspersed with cutting-edge technology. The echo of humanity's past intermingled with the hum of its future, a reminder of the remarkable journey they were all part of. Jenkins guided them to an elevator she stood outside of it, she motioned the group in. Once in the elevator, Jenkins swiped her access card through a sleek, high-tech panel. A soft, digital chime signaled approval, and the elevator smoothly ascended. The trio found themselves surrounded by a fully panoramic view as they steadily rose, each floor a hive of activity. Offices and meeting rooms, filled with people in various Federation uniforms, encircled the exterior of the elevator shaft. Some were huddled over interactive displays, others engaged in animated discussions, their gestures as impassioned as their debates. Bots whizzed through the hallways, delivering messages and items, their paths choreographed to avoid collisions. The Federation's insignia was seen everywhere, marking each piece of technology and decor with a unifying identity. As they ascended, the view changed from the close quarters of the lower floors to a sprawling vista of the complex itself. They could see the skyline of New York City, the shimmering East River, and the verdant expanse of Central Park, the island of Manhattan spread out beneath them in all its bustling, eco-futuristic glory.

The elevator slowed to a halt at the topmost floor, signaling their arrival at the uppermost echelons of Federation Command. The top floor was a stark contrast to the metallic, futuristic aesthetics they had seen below. It was lush and vibrant with greenery, interspersed with trees that reached up to touch the glass ceiling. Sunlight streamed in, dappling the floor with warm light, and creating a shifting tapestry of shadow and brightness. The top floor was also teeming with life of a different kind. Representatives from various galactic civilizations were scattered around the area, engaging in quiet discussions, observing the earthbound city below, or simply basking in the earthly sunlight. One group, in particular, stood out. They were members of the Erisians, an all-female species known for their radiant beauty and mind-reading abilities. They had an ethereal quality about them that was simultaneously enchanting and intimidating. McKinley was visibly taken aback, his eyes wide and mouth slightly ajar, as he took in the sight of the Erisians. Moore nudged him, pulling him back from his fascination. Leaning in close, she whispered, "They're Erisians. Known for their beauty, mind-reading abilities, and... well, their pansexual-panromantic orientation. They can reproduce with any species, which is quite unique." She added the last bit with a slight smile, finding McKinley's awe amusing. McKinley nodded, a new level of understanding and respect shining in his eyes for these enigmatic beings.

Jenkins' voice, calm and professional, broke through their conversation. She reported their arrival over her commutation device and gestured toward a large door on the opposite side of the room. "Command is waiting for you behind those doors," she said, her tone indicating that their journey was now at its end. The doors seemed unassuming, but the group knew that the people who waited behind them held the power to decide the course of the Federation's future. The trio approached the grand double doors of the command center, the Federation's insignia etched prominently on them. McKinley, however, was still engrossed by the sight of the Erisians. His gaze remained glued on them as he walked backward, tripping over his own feet. Reyes, noticing McKinley's distraction, cleared his throat and gave him a pointed look. "Eyes front, McKinley. Focus on the mission at hand." McKinley quickly turned around, his cheeks turning a faint pink under the mocking smiles of his companions. "Right, sorry boss," he mumbled, falling back in step with Reyes and Moore. Moore, who had been suppressing her smile, finally let it break free, a teasing glint in her eyes as she watched McKinley. McKinley shot her a sideways glance that clearly read 'not a word', but the smug smirk on Moore's face suggested that this was a story that would not be forgotten soon.

◆ ◆ ◆

The grand room was a visual spectacle, with an elevated platform where four figures stood, surveying the room from above. As the doors behind Reyes and his crew sealed shut, one of the figures stepped forward, his voice echoing in the vast expanse of the room.
"Captain Reyes," a voice called out. "Step forward."

Reyes responded promptly, leaving McKinley and Moore standing at attention as he moved to stand in front of the elevated platform. His posture was rigid, his arms tucked behind his back, and he wore a focused expression as he looked up at the four figures.
One by one, the commanding figures introduced themselves. The tall man, stern in countenance and with a gaze as piercing as a star's core, began.
"I am sure you know me Captain, I'm Admiral Lawson," he declared, his deep voice echoing in the grand room, "Fleet Commander of the Federation."
Next, a woman with a sharply contoured face, and icy eyes full of precision and calculation, stepped forward. "I'm Vice Admiral Nia Patel," she said, her voice crisp and clear, "Logistical Commander."
The third figure, a kindly faced man with an aura of tranquility and composed wisdom, introduced himself as "General Alfonso Diaz, Administrative Commander."
Finally, the fourth figure stepped into the light. A battle-hardened woman, her face etched with scars that bore testament to countless conflicts, announced herself with an almost tangible sense of pride and fortitude. "I am General Amelia Warner," she declared, her voice gruff yet steadfast, "Ground Commander of the Federation forces."
"Reyes," Admiral Lawson began, his voice filling the grand room. "You can stand at ease." Reyes nodded, shifting into a more

relaxed position but still maintaining a certain formal decorum. Lawson proceeded, "It's been a long time, Reyes. We are in a tight spot here. Your intel has been invaluable. This resurfacing of Stevens, though... it's not good." Lawson moved towards a massive display screen situated at one side of the room. With a swift hand motion, a detailed dossier of Stevens appeared on the screen, his face staring down at them with an inscrutable expression. Lawson began to explain, "Lynn Stevens, former Lieutenant of the Federation forces. An exceptionally talented officer, highly proficient in combat and tactics." He paused for a moment, his eyes scanning the document in front of him, "However, his increasing radicalism and disillusionment led to him going AWOL during the Mars Uprising. He disappeared for years, presumed dead... until now." "Now, about this weapon," Lawson moved to another section of the dossier, which displayed schematics of an advanced piece of technology. "It's not just a piece of technology. It's a weapon, a mountain buster, originally designed to aid our colonization efforts by easily reshaping terrains. If Stevens has it, he can cause unimaginable destruction." The room went quiet, the seriousness of the situation hanging heavy in the air. Everyone's eyes were on Lawson, waiting for his next words. Vice Admiral Nia Patel, the Logistical Commander, stepped forward, her gaze fixed on the schematics. "The weapon is known as the Terraformer," she began, her voice ringing out in the silence. "As the name suggests, it was designed to 'terraform' - to make uninhabitable worlds habitable. It uses advanced technology to reshape geological features - making mountains where there were none or eliminating them entirely." She pointed to a part of the schematics, a complex matrix of lines and shapes. "This here is the core of the weapon, an extremely powerful energy source that triggers geological changes. It works by instigating subterranean geological reactions which can cause land to rise or fall at an unprecedented scale. If used incorrectly, the Terraformer can lead to catastrophic destruction, it could devastate cities, even entire planets." A sobering silence followed her explanation. The threat posed by the Terraformer in the hands of Stevens was clear - it was a potential disaster of astronomical proportions. General Amelia Warner, the Ground Commander, leaned on the holographic table, her gaze unwavering as she addressed the room. Her roughened voice, textured by years of issuing orders in the heat of battle, spoke volumes about her experience. "Stevens, with the Terraformer, is not just a threat to cities or planets," she began, her words commanding attention, "He's a threat to our forces, the backbone of the Federation. Picture a battalion of our best, ready for battle, and suddenly, the very ground they stand on rises into a mountain or falls into a valley. No amount of training or weaponry can prepare you for the land itself turning against you." Her eyes met each person's gaze in the room, the severity of her message resonating clearly. "We'd lose not just ground, but countless lives, good soldiers. Our strategic advantage, our fortifications... useless. And if he were to target our larger installations, even our starships aren't safe. Imagine a starship crashing into an unexpected mountain or being swallowed by a sudden chasm. It's not just a weapon; in the wrong hands, it's the end of the Federation as we know it." With a solemn expression etched on his face, Reyes finally broke his silence. The room turned their attention to him as he began to outline his theory. "It is plausible," he began, his voice steady and determined, "that Stevens has taken advantage of the situation on Mars. Its breakaway from the Federation during our failed operation might be the key. I suspect he's used this to radicalize the planet." He paused for a moment, his gaze stern, before continuing. "He means to use this weapon on Earth. With Mars potentially under his sway and his proven capability to operate right under our noses - his base was on that moon, after all - it indicates he could now be anywhere within our systems." The room fell into a thick silence as they digested Reyes' theory. His words echoed, a stark reminder of the gravity of the situation they were facing. General Alfonso Diaz stepped forward, his posture rigid, but his eyes reflecting a certain weariness. He began speaking about the situation on Mars. "The Red Planet, as you know," he began, "has been in turmoil since its breakaway from the Federation. They have declared themselves the Martian Republic under a new leadership - a leadership that has, unfortunately, fostered anti-Federation sentiment amongst its populace." Diaz paused for a moment, his jaw tight. "We've had little success in establishing a dialogue with them. Their leader, a charismatic and enigmatic figure named Orion Vallis, has stoked the fires of independence and autonomy." His gaze met Reyes'. "And now, with your theory... It's a frightening thought that Mars could be a potential ally for Stevens. We need to tread very carefully here." "Of course, sir, it's just a theory," Reyes responded, locking eyes with General Diaz. His voice held a firmness that underlined his years of experience and countless trials faced as a captain. "But it's one that we cannot afford to ignore, given the stakes." "Reyes," Admiral Lawson began, his voice authoritative and steady, "your mission on that moon proves you're capable of handling this situation. I'm putting you in command of this operation." The room went quiet, every pair of eyes fixated on Reyes, who stood tall despite the sudden shift of responsibility. "You'll need a crew, and I'm assuming you can handle assembling one," Lawson continued, his gaze never leaving Reyes. "You'll have the full support of the Federation behind you." At this, the room seemed to exhale in unison, a palpable sense of relief washing over everyone. The Admiral was placing his trust in Reyes, and with it, the safety of the entire Federation. Lawson's gaze then shifted to General Diaz. "And as for a ship," he added, "General Diaz, see to it that Captain Reyes here is properly accommodated." Diaz saluted sharply, acknowledging the order. "Understood, sir," he responded, his voice echoing throughout the room. "You will have a ship, Captain Reyes." As Lawson's words settled, the weight of Reyes's new assignment began to truly sink in. He was tasked with the Federation's safety, with preventing a disaster of unimaginable scale. The trust and responsibility now resting on his shoulders were immense, but he was ready to rise to the challenge. Lawson fixed Reyes with a steady gaze as he continued, "Reyes, your mission now is to uncover what you can about Stevens. If he intends to use this weapon against Earth, we must ensure that his plans fail." Lawson's voice was grave, underlining the seriousness of their situation. "We're placing our trust in you," he added, "Commander Reyes." The silence that followed was deafening. The Admiral's words echoed through the room, leaving an almost tangible weight in their wake. Reyes was no longer just a Captain; he was now a Commander with the daunting task of safeguarding their home planet, Earth. Despite the enormity of his new responsibility, Reyes nodded firmly, ready to face the challenge head-on. Lawson paused for a moment, and then added, "Oh, and there's one more thing, Commander. There is a certain individual who could prove invaluable to your mission." "Dr. Aeesse M'doius," Lawson continued, pointing to a holographic image of an Erisian woman projected in the middle of the room. "She's an expert in a wide range of scientific fields, renowned across the galaxy. She also holds deep knowledge about ancient and long-forgotten civilizations." The hologram displayed a striking Erisian woman. Her presence, even as a holographic projection, was both captivating and intimidating. Her eyes seemed to hold the wisdom of countless centuries, and her face appeared to glow with an inner radiance. "She's currently on her home planet, Eridania, in the Orion Nebula," Lawson added. "We'll arrange for you to meet her. Having an Erisian on your team would certainly provide a unique perspective." Reyes considered this, the prospect of working with an Erisian was intriguing. The mysteries surrounding their species, coupled with their vast knowledge, would undoubtedly be invaluable in their mission.

CHAPTER 6

With a newfound sense of purpose, Reyes, McKinley, and Moore exited the room. Each step they took reverberated with the weight of their new mission, the safety of Earth and the entire Federation resting on their shoulders. Making their way back down the eco-futuristic building, the trio engaged in low, hushed conversations, discussing potential strategies, and sharing their thoughts on their recent promotion. Their dialogue was broken only by the occasional bursts of chatter from Federation officials passing by or the whirring of some distant piece of machinery. The trio found General Diaz waiting for them near the transport bay. His demeanor, previously serious and somewhat aloof, seemed to have softened slightly. He gestured for them to follow, leading the way towards the docking bay where their new ship, their new home for the foreseeable future, awaited.
"Commander!" Diaz exclaimed. "Your just in time for the show!" Just then, the docking bay began to hum with a distant mechanical energy, a chorus of dormant systems and silent machines. It was still and quiet—until a faint rumble began to vibrate the walls. The sound grew louder, morphing into a thunderous roar as a shadow washed over them. From above, the colossal form of a ship descended into view, its massive engines vibrating with a primal force that overwhelmed all

other sound. their ship had arrived. The ship was a magnificent sight, sleek and elongated, with a powerful presence that commanded attention. Its hull was dotted with a plethora of missile and laser batteries, promising a deadly force if provoked. The engines flanking its rear were monstrous, their power promising swift and decisive motion. General Diaz's proudly proclaimed, "Commander, meet the FSS Bushido RS1, the first of the Reconnaissance Stealth series. It's equipped with state-of-the-art stealth tech." Diaz gestured towards the vessel, a note of pride creeping into his voice. "Nothing or no one will ever see it coming, not even pirates."

"This is your ship, Commander Reyes," Diaz said, turning to look at Reyes with a gleam in his eye. "You will be its first Commander. Take good care of her, and she will take good care of you." There was a moment of silence as the weight of Diaz's words sank in. The responsibility was enormous, but so was the honor. As the first captain of a Reconnaissance Stealth ship, Reyes was not just making history; he was about to guide it. The thought was both thrilling and terrifying. Reyes stood awestruck, his gaze tracing the sleek lines and powerful form of the ship. He finally broke his silence, the words barely above a whisper, "Most Federation ships are bulky and sluggish... this thing... it's like a civilian sports shuttle." Mckinley, ever the source of levity, chipped in, "Bushido, huh? What's it going to do, commit seppuku if we lose a skirmish?" His light-hearted chuckle echoed around the massive docking bay, causing a few nearby crew members to stifle their own laughter. Diaz, although slightly taken aback by McKinley's irreverent humor, gave a smirk and shook his head. "Let's hope it never comes to that, McKinley," he replied, the slight twinkle in his eye showing his amusement. "But for now," Diaz continued, "let's get you acquainted with your new home." The pilot, a member of the Tranakaran race known as Syv, introduced themselves. The

Tranakar are noted for their ability to process and communicate information in a non-linear fashion, which often gave their speech a certain unorthodox, yet efficient cadence. "Greetings, Commander Reyes," Syv's voice rang out, modulated and precise, each word distinct. "Also, salutations Sergeant McKinley and First Lieutenant Moore. I am Flight Lieutenant Syv, your helm officer for this expedition." Reyes awkwardly extended his hand towards Syv, who returned the gesture as best they could with their webbed tri-digits. After a moment of adaptation, Reyes gave a brief nod of acknowledgment. "Lead the way," he said, gesturing towards the belly of the ship. As they began their ascent into the vessel, the trio took a moment to appreciate the marvel of technology into which they were stepping. This would be their home, their base, their sanctuary in the depths of space for the foreseeable future. And at its helm, an alien entity with a mind that ran on different tracks than their own. It was a daunting prospect, but also thrilling in its novelty. For McKinley, Moore, and their newly minted Commander, the journey was just beginning. "A tour is order." Syv said, displaying an intuitive understanding of the ship's layout, first led Reyes to the humming heart of the ship, the engine bay. With its Singular Energy Reactor thrumming softly with contained energy, it was a testament to advanced human and alien engineering. Moore, with a gleam in her eyes and a clear fascination for the technical marvel before her, broke away from the group. She was pulled, like a moth to the flame, towards the sleek panels and flickering lights that controlled this technological powerhouse.

Next, Syv ushered Reyes into the crew quarters - a space given over to comfort and personal solace. The layout was efficient, with each private room arranged neatly along a central hallway. While modest in size, each space was well-designed and offered privacy - a valued luxury on any spacecraft. As they walked into the area, McKinley let out a low whistle of astonishment, a broad grin lighting up his face. "These quarters are fancier than I reckoned!" he exclaimed in his unique accent, clearly pleased with the accommodations. He winked at Reyes and Syv, his eyes twinkling with mischief before he added, "Might just be the best place to hide me bottles of whisky!" With a guffaw echoing down the corridor, McKinley retreated into the room nearest to the common area, his laughter still hanging in the air as the door slid shut behind him. That left Reyes alone with Syv, as they continued their tour towards the nerve center of the Bushido—the bridge. The elongated chamber was dominated by a Command Information Center (CIC) in the middle, with a holographic display of the Milky Way galaxy rotating serenely above it. Points of light flickered on its surface, marking plotted destinations, known hazards, and points of interest. Syv gestured to it with a slight bobbing motion, a quirk of their species. "Commander, this is the nerve center of the Bushido," Syv said, their voice carrying an undertone of pride. "The galaxy map here is directly linked with the Federation's latest data feeds, offering real-time strategic information." Reyes studied the display, his eyes tracking the moving points of light. He wondered what adventures and challenges each of those points might hold for his new crew. But most importantly, which one would lead them to Stevens. Wrapping up the tour, Syv guided Reyes to the intricate communications system installed within the ship. "Commander, you can use this to send and receive messages to anyone, anytime," the Tranakar informed, gesturing to the sleek array of consoles. "Just touch this panel here to initiate a new message, and this one to retrieve received messages. And if you require me, I'll be stationed at the ship's controls." Syv then pointed to a staircase that led to an upper level. "Your Captain's Quarters are located up there. They're equipped with all you might need for rest and solitude." Syv's voice carried a note of finality as they concluded, "If you're not planning on resting, feel free to chart our course on the Command Information Center in the bridge. Whenever you're ready, Commander, we'll set off!" Reyes now speaking. "Thanks Syv for your wonderful tour." He paused thinking about his next words. "Now that you mention it, I think I will take myself a quick nap, it's been a long day." Syv acknowledged with a nod and final words "Understood Commander, I'll be here when you're ready to set off." With that, Syv left the commander to explore his new quarters.

◆ ◆ ◆

These quarters were significantly larger than what Reyes was accustomed to, even for a high-ranking officer. A gentle, ambient light flooded the room through a skylight, casting the furniture in a soothing glow. His bed, a grand king-sized fixture, sat in the center of the room, beckoning with the promise of comfort and rest. He changed into a comfortable sleeping outfit and then positioned himself on the bed, lying back against the soft pillows. He looked up through the skylight, his gaze resting on the rolling clouds of Earth high above. It was a sight that filled him with a sense of tranquility, anchoring him to the world he was sworn to protect. As he drifted off to sleep, the last thing he saw was the beautiful swirling mists of the Earth's atmosphere, the planet's natural shield and blanket. His slumber, while initially peaceful, was soon marred by a chilling nightmare. He was back on the moon, his astral form hovering high above The Undaunting as it tumbled helplessly toward the surface. The horrifying spectacle of the ship tearing a ruinous path across the lunar surface was punctuated by the echoing screams of the crew. Suddenly, his vision was filled with flashes of Stevens. His face was contorted in a menacing laugh, his eyes gleaming with cold triumph. The image of the man who had caused so much destruction and pain was etched into his nightmare, branding his sleep with the scars of that fateful mission. Reyes jerked awake with a start, his heart pounding in his chest. The tranquil image of the Earth's rolling clouds still visible through his skylight was a stark contrast to the nightmare he'd just escaped from. He was back in reality, but the echoes of his dream still lingered, a chilling reminder of the task that lay ahead of him.

CHAPTER 7

Reyes, filled with a renewed sense of purpose after his unsettling dream, swiftly dressed himself and made his way down to the bridge. As he descended the stairs, he was greeted by Moore, her eyes sparkling with excitement. "Commander, you won't believe it," she began, her words tumbling out in a rush. "This ship is nothing short of incredible. The technology, the design - it's light-years ahead of anything we've used before." Her enthusiasm was infectious, and Reyes found himself smiling despite the urgency of their situation. The awe-inspiring capabilities of their new vessel provided a spark of hope amidst their daunting mission. Reyes inquired. "First Lieutenant Moore, glad to see you made it up here, please enlighten me on what you've discovered." Moore's face lit up as she began to explain. "Well, Commander, this is a veritable marvel of technology. The heart of the ship - the Singular Energy Reactor - is capable of generating enough energy to power a small colony. It's the primary reason why we can support such a sophisticated stealth system, and simultaneously run all ship operations with power to spare. I've never seen anything like it." She continued, excitement evident in her voice. "The hull is constructed with a new material that's lighter than any known metal yet stronger than anything we've got in the Federation fleet. It's designed for maximum maneuverability, allowing us to outflank any threat we might encounter." Moore then gestured towards the control panel. "The interface, Commander, is so intuitive that even McKinley should be able to handle it with minimal training. And the CIC's 3D map of the Milky Way - it's as detailed as any star chart in existence, with the added bonus of real-time data on celestial movements." She paused, a smile tugging at her lips. "And the living quarters! Space might be a premium on most vessels, but not here. Every crew member gets their own personal space to modify as they see fit. It's a touch of 'home' that's sorely missing on most missions." All in all, Moore's description painted the FSS Bushido RS1 as a cutting-edge piece of technology, designed for both comfort and functionality, and their key advantage in the mission ahead. Reyes was visibly impressed by Moore's analysis of the ship. He looked at her, his gaze steady and confident, and spoke with an air of certainty. "See, that's why you're here, Moore. I'm putting you in charge of commanding the operations throughout the ship. We need to make sure this ship runs efficiently and effectively every day," he stated firmly. Moore's eyes widened, and her initial reaction was one of disbelief. She hadn't expected to be entrusted with such an important responsibility so quickly. Regaining her composure, she stood straight and nodded. "Aye, Commander. I will ensure everything is in order," she said with a mix of gratitude and determination in her voice. Reyes gave her a reassuring smile. "I know you will. We've got a lot ahead of us, and I can't think of anyone better to have my back. Now, let's get this mission started." With renewed vigor, the two made their way to the Command Information Center to start plotting their course. The FSS Bushido RS1 was about to embark on a mission that could determine the fate of the Earth and the entire Federation.

◆ ◆ ◆

Standing on the platform overlooking the Command Information Center (CIC), Reyes took a moment to marvel at the interactive 3D map of the Milky Way galaxy. With a simple sweep of his hand, he navigated the intricate star map towards the Erisian homeworld, Eridania. A vibrant blue world glowing brilliantly in the holographic display, located in the mesmerizing expanse of the Orion Nebula. He turned to Syv, the Flight Lieutenant, and spoke with an air of command, "Flight Lieutenant Syv, set our course for Eridania in the Orion Nebula. We're going to recruit Dr. Aeesse M'doius. Her knowledge will be invaluable to our efforts."

Syv, processing the Commander's orders, responded promptly in his robotic-like tone, "Aye, Commander. Setting course for Eridania." As the coordinates were inputted, the stars on the holographic map shifted to align with their new destination. The anticipation of the journey ahead filled the room. This was the beginning of their mission, a quest for answers and a fight for their world. Unlike traditional Federation vessels with their warp drives, the FSS Bushido RS1 utilized a more advanced, cutting-edge propulsion method. Its technology was designed to project a stable wormhole in front of the ship, bridging the vast distances of space by creating a direct pathway to their destination. From the ship's bridge, Reyes and Moore watched in awe as the space before them distorted, twisting, and contorting as the wormhole came into existence. A vibrant swirl of blues and purples, the wormhole was a stunning, celestial phenomena that stood as a testament to the marvels of modern technology. As the ship began to move, the edges of the wormhole seemed to pull inward, swallowing the Bushido into its cosmic tunnel. The scene was breathtaking, a moment where time seemed to suspend, and the spectacle of the cosmos was laid bare before them. Moore turned to Reyes, her face illuminated by the otherworldly glow. She grinned, a sense of excitement and trepidation visible in her eyes. Reyes gave a reassuring nod, silently acknowledging the gravity of their mission and the groundbreaking journey they had embarked on. Syv, with his characteristic calm demeanor, turned towards Reyes and Moore. His voice carried a soothing monotone as he assured them of the safety of wormhole travel. "I have been part of the Bushido's test flights," he stated, his antennae twitching slightly. "I can assure you with full confidence that the system works perfectly. Our journey will be smooth and uneventful." Even as he spoke, reality seemed to distort around them. It was as if time itself was bending, twisting into impossible shapes. It was a feeling akin to vertigo, but without any accompanying discomfort. It was merely a disconcerting sensation that was over as quickly as it had begun. And then, suddenly, they were elsewhere. The star system Aviran sprawled before them, its celestial bodies strewn like jewels against the canvas of space. Among them, a pale greenish-purple sphere of a planet hung in the distance. Its surface was marred by white swirls of storm systems, creating a mesmerizing pattern on its face. "That," Syv said, pointing one of his three-fingered hands at the planet, "is Eridania. Our destination." There was a certain solemnity to his tone, acknowledging the gravity of their mission as they approached the Erisian home world.

◆ ◆ ◆

Within the gravity well of Eridania now, the awe-inspiring vista of the planet expanded before their eyes. Joined now by Mckinley, the trio watched as an imposing Erisian battle fleet filled their view. The vessels came in various shapes and sizes, but one stood out among them, demanding their attention.
At the heart of the fleet was an immense triangle-shaped ship, its form smooth and seamless, a titan among the stars. Its sheer size dwarfed the surrounding vessels, standing as a testament to

Erisian might and technological prowess. Syv's eyes, fixed on the massive battle cruiser, narrated its identity to his companions. "That," he said, pointing a three-fingered hand at the massive vessel, "is the Tempest. The largest battle cruiser known in the systems. Rumors in the stellar lanes speak of its crew numbering in the tens of thousands." His voice carried a hint of awe, not simply for the intimidating presence of the Erisian ship but for what it represented: the advanced technology and military strength of the Erisian civilization. It was an imposing sight, one that would give pause to even the most seasoned of space travelers. A communication request pinged on the Bushido's system, the caller ID registering as the colossal Erisian vessel, Tempest. Syv promptly answered the call, his voice steady "This is the FSS Bushido our intentions are peaceful, we in search of a one, Dr. Aeesse M'doius" A deep, resonant voice from the Tempest responded, its tone carrying the weight of authority. "You are granted permission to proceed to Lysithea," the voice said, referring to the gleaming Erisian capital city nestled on the planet's surface, known for its beautiful architectural marvels and breathtaking landscapes. "Maintain your current course and speed. You will be escorted upon reaching the planetary atmosphere." Acknowledging their directive, Syv promptly relayed the coordinates to the ship's navigation system. Their journey to Eridania had officially begun.

CHAPTER 8

As the FSS Bushido cut through the cloud cover, the group was met with the astonishing sight of Lysithea, the ancient Erisian city. Age-old structures, a blend of regal elegance and high-tech design, stretched as far as the eye could see. Syv, who was piloting the ship, provided a running commentary on the sights. "The Erisians are the oldest existing civilization in the galaxy," he noted, a hint of awe in his usually composed tone. Moore, ever the inquisitive scientist, caught on to his words. "Existing?" she echoed, questioning the implication. "Well, there have always been rumors of civilizations that predate the Erisians," Syv admitted, his focus remaining on the navigation ahead. "Some Erisian scholars are believed to have concrete evidence of these past civilizations, but such knowledge is kept hidden. Perhaps Dr. Aeesse M'doius can shed some light on this for you."

"Makes you think of those ancient humans, doesn't it?" Mckinley chimed in, a mischievous glint in his eyes. "Thought the whole bloody universe revolved around 'em." His remark drew a round of laughter from the group, dispelling some of the tension that had built up during their descent. Even Syv seemed to appreciate the jest, his synthesized tone almost conveying amusement. "Indeed, Lieutenant McKinley," the alien pilot acknowledged, his strange accent softening McKinley's rough-hewn humor. "It is common for younger species to consider themselves the center of the universe. Humility comes with age and wisdom." The comment seemed to resonate with the group, each member lost in their own thoughts as they pondered the vast history of civilizations before them. It was a humbling realization that added to the weight of their mission and their place in the grand scheme of things.

◆ ◆ ◆

"We're coming into land now, please prepare," Syv's modulated voice echoed through the ship. Establishing communication with ground control, he was swiftly given permission to dock at one of the city's numerous landing pads. Despite the Bushido's substantial size, Syv piloted the ship with impressive finesse, guiding the spacecraft to a gentle landing. The ship made a soft thud as the landing gears absorbed the impact, with the sound of magnetic devices latching onto the hull echoing throughout the ship. This subtle cacophony signaled that they were securely anchored to the landing pad. "Welcome to Lysithea, everyone," Syv announced once they were safely landed. He quickly pulled up a holographic map of the city, highlighting a few areas. "The university district is likely where you'll find Dr. M'doius, either in her lab or possibly one of the many ancient history libraries. The Erisians take their knowledge keeping very seriously." His words were met with nods of understanding from Reyes and his crew, ready to embark on this next phase of their mission. The group prepared themselves for disembarking, Reyes gathered his team for a quick briefing. "The Erisians are well respected within the Federation," he started, "We should make sure to show them the best side of humanity while we're here. That especially goes for you, McKinley. I know how much you enjoy your whisky." From the cockpit, Syv chimed in, his voice carrying a note of amusement, "Good thing there isn't whisky on this planet. Local spirits only, some not suitable for non-Erisian consumption, might I add." Mckinley looked slightly annoyed at the exchange, muttering something under his breath before looking at Reyes and replying more audibly, "Aye, Commander." Turning to Moore, Reyes continued, "Moore, try to contain your curiosity to a tolerable level. We're here to meet Dr. M'doius and gather information, not ruffle feathers with a barrage of questions." Moore, barely looking up from the gadget she was fiddling with, gave a small smirk, "No promises, Commander, but I'll do my best." Finally, Reyes addressed Syv, "Syv, keep the ship ready for immediate departure. We don't know what we're walking into and it's always wise to have an exit strategy." "Understood, Commander," Syv acknowledged with a nod. Once the brief was concluded, they stepped off the ship, their boots touching the alien soil of Lysithea, ready to start their mission. An Erisian envoy was waiting for them. She was tall, even by Erisian standards, with shimmering violet skin that seemed to reflect different colors under Lysithea's sky. Her bright, opalescent eyes flicked back and forth between the landing craft and her surroundings, as if expecting danger to present itself at any moment. As the team stepped off the ship, she hurried over to them. "I am Lyra," she introduced herself, her voice like the soft hum of a musical instrument. "I serve as an intermediary to Governor Illiana. The Tempest relayed your arrival, and she has been informed." Commander Reyes stepped forward, extending his hand in the traditional human gesture of greeting. "Commander Reyes," he introduced himself. Then he gestured to his companions, "This is First Officer Moore, our chief scientist, and Sergeant McKinley, security officer." Each member of his team nodded in acknowledgment as they were introduced. "Greetings" touching her chest with a palm. "Commander Reyes." Lyra paused, Reyes tilted his head slightly to listen in closer. "Illiana would like to formally invite you and your crew, she wishes to speak of an important matter, one she deems suited for, the honorable, Commander Reyes." She then gestured for them to follow her into the city, and they fell into step behind her, their mission on Eridania officially underway. Reyes nodded in understanding as the group continued following Lyra, their path winding through the heart of Lysithea. They moved through bustling streets, past structures that spanned the gap between the ancient and modern, each embodying the long, storied history of the Erisians and their advances in technology. Despite their own technological prowess, the members of the team couldn't help but be awed by the profound sense of history and progress that permeated Eridania.

◆ ◆ ◆

Lyra led the group towards an expansive circular district. Buildings radiating an aura of importance and power surrounded them. The grand architecture was a striking blend of antiquity and futurism, with soaring towers that merged seamlessly with advanced technology. They were heading into the heart of the Civitas district, the political hub of Erisian society. "Commander Reyes," Lyra spoke up, her eyes on the imposing structure in the center of the district. "This is the Civitas. It's the heart of Erisian governance, knowledge, and diplomacy. All paths here lead to the Aegis Spire," she gestured toward the tallest structure among them. It was a breathtaking monument that touched the very clouds. Bridges of various sizes stretched from the Aegis Spire to the surrounding buildings, serving as veins that pulsed with the lifeblood of Erisian politics. "You will meet Governor Illiana within the Aegis Spire," Lyra concluded, pointing to the central building before leading them towards it. As they navigated the vast corridors, Lyra couldn't help but break the silence, her gaze subtly glancing back at Reyes. "Commander," she began, her voice echoing off the tall, grand walls adorned with ancient Erisian artifacts hanging suspended in the air. "That ship of yours is quite a marvel. A human vessel capable of wormhole generation. Your people are surely on the brink of a new era, a golden age, if you will."

She turned her gaze forward again, her eyes glittering with a peculiar mixture of respect and curiosity. Despite their architectural and cultural grandeur, the Erisians were not a species to dismiss technological advancement, especially one as pivotal as wormhole generation. Moore, appreciative of Lyra's admiration, agreed, "Indeed, the singularity energy is in its infancy. We are still discovering new applications and possibilities. It's quite a rapid evolution, even for us." Just then, McKinley, ever the source of amusement, chimed in, "Aye, don't forget the human element. We've got a right knack for surprising ourselves and the universe." At this, Lyra chuckled, her stoic Erisian composure giving way to arrogance, She raised an eyebrow at McKinley, her tone light, "Ah, the human bravado, indeed. It's quite the staple in your kind's reputation, isn't it, McKinley?" McKinley slightly annoyed at this point began to turn red in the face. He started to speak. "I'll have you kno..." just then Reyes reached over and jabbed Mckinley in his ribs with his elbow. Reyes spoke with just his lips the word "STOP" was seen by McKinley, he nodded, and his eyes expressed his apologies.

◆ ◆ ◆

As they approached a location that bore the hallmarks of an elevator, Lyra surprised the group. She gestured for them to come close. When they complied, she closed her eyes, and her face took on an ethereal stillness. Moments later, her eyes flicked open, not the usual vibrant blue, but now a piercing, luminescent white. Without warning, the surroundings blurred, shifting and warping. It was an experience akin to being in a wormhole, but more localized, more intimate. In less than the blink of an eye, they found themselves standing in an entirely new location. As quickly as it had begun, the disorientation ceased. Lyra's eyes returned to their normal hue as she gently came out of her trance-like state. She turned to face the group, a knowing smile on her face. The expressions of the humans ranged from startled surprise to bewildered fascination. Despite their vast experiences in space, they were unaccustomed to such personal, immediate teleportation. Lyra chuckled lightly, "Welcome to Erisian transportation."

Continuing on, Lyra began to explain further. "We Erisians have a unique capability – the ability to teleport through the sheer force of our minds, manipulating the fabric of space-time itself at our whim," she said, her voice radiating a sense of pride. "You might refer to it as a form of telekinesis or psionics." "It's an integral part of our culture, our way of life," she continued. "While we have the technology for conventional transport, nothing can quite replicate the convenience and immediacy of personal teleportation. Of course, such abilities require rigorous training and discipline to harness effectively, and not all Erisians choose to cultivate them." The human team listened with a mix of awe and intrigue. This was a glimpse into an aspect of Erisian life that was not widely known outside their world, a culture that melded advanced technology with innate psychic abilities in a manner unique to their species. This encounter was rapidly broadening their understanding of the galaxy's diversity, hinting at even more to learn and discover in their mission. Reyes usually composed and professional responded with a sense of awe. "That's most impressive Lyra, humanity would benefit greatly from such powers, a ship without doors, now that would make an enemy think twice before boarding." "You're right, Commander Reyes. It's indeed a remarkable ability," Lyra responded, her voice touched with a hint of pride. "And you're correct in stating that such powers could be advantageous to humanity. However, it's important to note that psionic abilities aren't exclusive to Erisians. They are inherent in all lifeforms to varying extents, waiting to be awakened. Yet, for most species, this awakening often takes millennia. Even we Erisians are restricted to local teleportation. Now, let's not dwell on this. Our esteemed governor, Governor Illiana, awaits us. She's not someone you'd want to keep waiting." With that, she gracefully steered them towards the Governor's office, ready to introduce them to the leader of her people.

◆ ◆ ◆

As they neared the governor's office, the hum of the city grew louder, a testament to the bustling metropolis. Lyra motioned for the group to enter, and they stepped into a spacious office that offered a panoramic view of the city. Transparent floor-to-ceiling walls made it feel as if the city itself was part of the room, the ceaseless movement of aerial vehicles both above and below adding to its vibrancy. Standing by the grand window, her back turned towards them, stood Illiana. She was tall, with a regal aura about her that demanded respect. Her skin glowed a gentle lavender, a common trait amongst Erisians, and her elongated silver hair shimmered under the ambient light. Robes of deep emerald, green draped over her, the intricate gold embroidery a symbol of her high standing. Illiana's hands were clasped behind her back as she stared out at the city. Without turning around, she acknowledged their presence, her voice smooth, soothing yet authoritative. "Ah, Commander Reyes," she said, her voice ringing through the room like a melodic song. "It's good to finally meet you. I have something that I believe only a person of your talents could handle." She turned around, her intense, violet eyes meeting those of Commander Reyes, indicating the gravity of what was about to be discussed.

CHAPTER 9

Illiana gracefully extended her hand, indicating to the luxurious seats arranged around a holographic table. The commander and his team took their seats, their attention completely focused on her. "There's a matter of grave concern threatening the peace and stability of our space," she began, her face a mask of controlled concern. "A faction of Erisians, dissatisfied with the current order, has recently emerged. They've managed to obtain an ancient device - a relic of a long-forgotten era. Its power is... immense, capable of altering the very fabric of spacetime." A hologram flickered into existence above the table, showing a device of alien design, intricate and enigmatic. "We believe they aim to use this device to open a rift, a doorway, into a parallel universe. We don't know what lies on the other side, but the consequences could be catastrophic, not just for Erisians, but for the entire galaxy."

The room fell silent as the weight of her words settled in. Reyes, breaking the silence, agreed to aid them, his voice steady, "We'll do everything in our power to prevent this catastrophe. In return, we request that Dr. M'doius accompany us on our mission, once the crisis is resolved." Illiana, relief washing over her features, nodded her agreement, "You have our gratitude, Commander. Dr. M'doius will be at your disposal once this ordeal is over. But for now, we must focus on stopping this faction and securing the device. We've been unable to locate their base of operations, and time is running short." Illiana watched as a jolt of energy surged through Commander Reyes at the mention of Stevens. "He was here on Eridania," she said carefully, measuring her words. "He sought an audience with the governing council under the guise of diplomacy. No one suspected him of any ill intentions until we were alerted by the Galactic Federation of his crimes." Reyes stood up, his face tight with tension, "Where is he now?!" "We don't know," Illiana said, matching his urgency. "He departed suddenly after his audience, and our security forces have been on high alert ever since. We have every available agent trying to track his movements, but as of now, we have no leads." Reyes clenched his fists, a wave of frustration passing over him. "That man is dangerous," he said, his voice hard. "He's a threat to every living being in this galaxy." "We understand," Illiana replied, her gaze sympathetic yet firm. "And we are doing everything in our power to find him. We will not let his evil spread in Erisian space." His voice layered with resolve, Reyes paced toward the windows, his gaze lost in the distant cityscape. "With Stevens here, and the situation you described, there has to be a correlation. It can't just be a coincidence," he stated firmly. His words hung heavily in the air, a tense silence following his declaration. Moore, her analytical mind quickly piecing together the puzzle, turned to Illiana. "This device of yours, capable of opening gateways to other realms... what could be there of such significance that Stevens would want it?" she inquired. Her tone was filled with a mix of concern and curiosity, her eyes searching Illiana's for answers. "We can't waste any time," Reyes interjected urgently. He swiftly moved from the window to face Illiana directly. "Tell us where this faction is located, Illiana." Illiana paused momentarily before answering, her tone steady. "They have taken up residence in the Torma Caverns, on the outskirts of the city." His determination mounting, Reyes immediately turned to his crew, "We need to prepare, gear up. We're heading out. We have to confront this faction before Stevens does or moves them his cause." His voice echoed in the room, the urgency in his tone was evident - every second was now crucial. Reyes and the group were on their way out, Illiana called out, "Commander, I'll send for Dr. Aeesse M'doius, the one you seek. She's an expert on Erisian factions and the psionic device. She can provide invaluable insight. I'll have her meet you on your ship." Pausing at the door, Reyes turned back to look at Illiana. His expression was serious, yet there was a glint of appreciation in his eyes. "Your generosity won't be forgotten, Governor. We'll do everything we can to resolve this situation." With that, he stepped out of the room, his team following closely, their faces etched with determination. They were ready for the challenge ahead.

◆ ◆ ◆

Back on the ship now, the group was gearing up for battle, donning armored suits and grabbing weapons. Syv's voice came over Reyes' communication device, "Dr. Aeesse M'dious is here, Commander. Also, Illiana has prepared a shuttle for your crew whenever you are ready." "Thanks, Syv. Have the doctor meet us on the bridge," Reyes responded. As they made their way to the bridge, a figure emerged from the hallway. The Erisian was tall, with slender limbs and pale blue scales that seemed to change hue under different angles of light. Four large, almond-shaped eyes looked at them curiously. She wore what appeared to be an amalgamation of science and tradition in her attire. "I presume you are Commander Reyes," she spoke with a soft, melodic voice. "I am Dr. Aeesse M'dious. Governor Illiana informed me of your predicament, and I am here to lend my expertise." Reyes gave a respectful nod. "Welcome aboard the Bushido Doctor. This is First Officer Moore and Sergeant McKinley," he gestured towards his crew members. Moore and McKinley both nodded in greeting. "Let's not waste any time," Reyes said firmly. "Dr. M'dious, we were told that you might have some information on the faction that Governor Illiana mentioned, as well as the device they're after." Dr. M'dious began by explaining the faction's background. "The faction calls itself the 'Sentinels of the Gateway'. They're Erisian radicals who believe in the prophecy of the Ancients, which tells of a device, a 'Gateway', that could open doors to other worlds, other realities. Most Erisians regard this as mythology, but the Sentinels, they believe it's not only real but that it's their sacred duty to activate it." She paused, her eyes scanning each face in the room. "The 'Gateway', according to the prophecy, is said to be in a place of 'eternal twilight', which many interpret to mean the 'Shadowlands', a region on our world that's permanently shrouded in darkness due to its geographical positioning." Moore raised an eyebrow. "And this device... what's it supposed to do?" Dr. M'dious adjusted her eyepiece once more, the uncertainty visible in her eyes. "That's the thing. The prophecy is quite vague on that. It states that the Gateway 'opens the way to the beyond, revealing knowledge unseen and power untapped.' Some believe it's a pathway to enlightenment, a source of limitless energy, or even a portal to a parallel universe." Reyes leaned forward, interest piqued. "And Stevens is involved in this because...?" The doctor sighed. "We can only speculate, but given his recent activities, it's likely he's after the power the Gateway is purported to possess. If it's indeed a source of limitless energy or a portal to another universe, think of the potential for exploitation." The room fell into a tense silence. If the faction and Stevens managed to activate the Gateway and it did possess the power they suspected, the implications could be catastrophic. The balance of power across the galaxy could shift dramatically and unpredictably. There was also the danger of what could potentially come through such a portal if it indeed led to another universe. The threats were too enormous to contemplate. Reyes broke the silence. "We can't let that happen. We need to get to this 'Gateway' before they do and secure it." His voice was steady, his gaze unwavering. The mission had become even more critical. Reyes stopped at the threshold of the room, turning back to look at his crew. His eyes were hard, but behind them lay a wellspring of determination and resolve. "We stand on the precipice of something vast and uncharted," he began, his voice steady and composed. "I look at each of you and I see more than just skilled specialists, more than just members of my crew. I see a family, bound not by blood, but by a shared purpose, a common goal." He pointed towards the starscape visible through the nearby viewing port. "Out there is the unknown. The possible dangers, the potential rewards. We are venturing into a place few have tread before. There are no maps, no guides to what we might encounter. All we have is each other." His gaze swept over each person present, locking onto their eyes, making them feel seen, acknowledged. "The task ahead of us is daunting. We're not just battling a rogue operative or a radical faction. We're fighting for the balance of power in our galaxy, and possibly others. We're safeguarding life as we know it." Reyes paused, letting the weight of his words sink in. He then continued, his voice imbued with quiet intensity. "But know this - there isn't another group of people in the universe that I'd want at my side. I trust each of you implicitly. And I ask that you place that same trust in me." His gaze turned to the vast expanse of space outside once more. "This mission may test us in ways we've never been tested before. It will require all our strength, all our courage. But remember, we're a team. We look out for each other. We're united. And together, there's nothing we can't overcome." Reyes clenched his fist, setting his jaw. "Now let's get out there and do what we do best." The room fell silent for a moment before erupting into determined nods and murmurs of agreement. Syv, despite his AI nature, couldn't help but feel inspired by Reyes' words, his coding buzzing with renewed purpose.

◆ ◆ ◆

The group on the shuttle now, it's compact interior was bathed in the cool, ethereal light of the holographic projector as it displayed a detailed map of a remote area of Eridania. Jagged mountains and dense forests dominated the region, with a large, heavily fortified compound clearly marked as the focal point. Various other structures and locations in the vicinity were highlighted as well, each with a different set of coordinates. Reyes, standing tall and resolute, gestured to the hologram. "Our main objective is here," he pointed to the large compound, "This is where our intelligence indicates the device is located. It's heavily fortified and likely crawling with hostile forces." He then moved his hand to the smaller, scattered points on the map. "These are secondary objectives: ammo dumps, communication hubs, potential sleeping quarters. We cause as much disruption as we can, it'll confuse them and thin out their defenses around the primary target." Reyes turned to Moore. "Moore, you'll be on tech. Find that device and cripple any defenses or traps they might have set up around it." Next, he addressed McKinley. "Mckinley, your expertise in demolition and tactical diversions will be invaluable here. I want you to concentrate on disrupting their infrastructure." Looking at Dr. M'doius, he said, "Doctor, you're our resident expert on this device. As soon as we have it, I need you to inspect it and start working on how we can neutralize it." Lastly, Reyes pointed to his own marker on the hologram, located near the main objective. "I'll lead the main assault on the central compound. I'll be the distraction we need." He looked around at his crew, meeting their eyes in the dimly lit shuttle. "This isn't going to be easy, but we've faced down worse. We're not just doing this for ourselves or for the Erisians - we're doing this for the whole galaxy. Let's move out." The team responded affirmatively, each member acknowledging their roles. As the shuttle hummed with energy and started its descent towards the rugged Eridanian landscape, they mentally prepared for the intense conflict ahead.

CHAPTER 10

The shuttle pilot spoke out. "Approaching the drop zone Commander, two minutes." her hands tapping away at the monitors.
Reyes responded "Roger, team get ready, we don't know what we are getting into, prepare for anything."
Without warning the pilot yelled. "No way, we've got a missile lock, missile inbound! Commander you better grab hold of something back there!" Soon after, the shuttle was rocked by an explosion the engines could be heard winding down, their shuttle had just become a rock, plummeting through the atmosphere, its hull rattling and shaking. The pilot's voice was tense but controlled as she radioed in their status.
"This is Talon One! We've been hit and are going down, repeat, we are going down!" Reyes, still gripping a safety handle, turned his head towards Dr. M'dious. "Secure yourself! Use the emergency restraints!" he shouted over the cacophony of warning alarms.
Dr. M'dious, with remarkable calm, swiftly anchored herself with the safety harness.
Meanwhile, McKinley was less composed. "Fuckin'ell this is gonna hurt," he yelled, as he wrestled to find something to hold onto.
As the ground rapidly approached, the pilot managed to fire

retro thrusters, which slowed their descent marginally but not enough to prevent a rough crash landing. The shuttle hit the ground with a thunderous boom, skidding through dense foliage and coming to an abrupt halt against a cluster of rocks. Silence enveloped the interior of the shuttle as dust and smoke filled the air. The emergency lights flickered, providing scant illumination.

Reyes, shaken but undeterred, was the first to move. He unbuckled himself and went to check on the others. "Report! Is everyone okay?!" he shouted. Moore groaned but gave a thumbs-up. McKinley was sprawled over a storage locker, looking dazed, but he nodded as well. Dr. M'dious seemed remarkably unharmed and was already disconnecting herself from the safety harness. The pilot, sadly, was not responsive. Her sacrifice had likely saved the rest of them.

Reyes took a deep breath and turned to his team. "We're on foot from here. We need to move quickly. We can't let that device fall into the wrong hands and they know we are here." he commanded with resolve. They gathered what gear they could salvage from the wreck and started making their way through the dense forest, heading toward the location that was indicated on their map. Though their entry was anything but stealthy, Reyes knew they had a mission to complete. This was no longer just about solving a mystery; it was a race against time to prevent a potentially catastrophic event. The dense foliage and jagged landscape provided some measure of cover as the team advanced towards the enemy fortification. Plasma bolts zipped through the air, leaving scorching trails in their wake. Despite the intensity of the situation, Reyes noted that the incoming fire was surprisingly sparse. It was as if the enemy was spread thin, or perhaps they were simply underprepared for an attack. Moore, equipped with a sniper rifle, stayed back providing cover fire, picking off any enemy combatants he could spot. McKinley and Reyes pressed forward, using trees and rocks as cover, while returning fire whenever possible. Dr. M'dious, though unarmed, followed close behind, her knowledge about the device and the faction being essential to the mission. As they advanced, the initial rush of enemy fire began to dwindle. "They're falling back!" McKinley yelled over the sound of gunfire.

Reyes, taking advantage of the lull, motioned for his team to move up. "Push forward, keep your eyes peeled. Remember, we're not just here to fight, we're here to secure that device." They moved swiftly, utilizing the temporary confusion amongst the enemy ranks. They darted from cover to cover, their footsteps muffled by the thick undergrowth. As they neared the fortification, the true scale of the enemy base came into view. It was sprawling, with various structures and facilities scattered around. The question that lingered in the back of Reyes' mind was why was there such limited resistance? They were prepared for an uphill battle, but this was almost too easy. As they pressed on, ready to face whatever lies ahead, they could only hope that they weren't walking into a trap. Their mission and the fate of many depended on it. They approached the main entrance two massive doors lay ahead locked tight. Swiftly Moore tapped into the enemy's security system, her nimble fingers dancing over the holographic interface projected from her wrist-mounted device. She bypassed their firewalls and encryptions with relative ease, testament to his expertise. Once she gained control, the formidable, heavily fortified doors began to grind open, revealing the darkness of the base within. The team took a defensive position, hidden behind nearby structures, their eyes trained on the steadily widening entrance. They anticipated any possible outgoing fire, but none came. The base was eerily quiet, only the echoing grumble of the doors disturbed the silence.

Once the doors fully opened, the team regrouped, forming a tight unit. With a quick nod from Reyes, they pressed forward, their senses heightened, each step calculated. The dim, artificial light from inside the base cast long, menacing shadows as they stepped in, their eyes scanning the area for any signs of movement. McKinley was in front, his weapon raised, ready for any sudden encounters. Dr. M'dious stayed in the middle, protected by Reyes and Moore on either side. Stepping deeper into the base, they noticed that it was strangely devoid of enemy combatants. They moved cautiously, their boots echoing off the cold, metallic walls. They knew they were in the belly of the beast. Now, it was all about finding the device and getting out alive.

◆ ◆ ◆

Further into the compound, they found themselves in sporadic firefights with scattered groups of guards. Each confrontation, although swiftly dealt with, was a stark reminder of the danger they were in. But the sight that greeted them in the core of the base left them momentarily awestruck. The space was vast, its ceiling towering and lost in darkness, supported by colossal, ancient columns. At its heart stood the monolithic device, an imposing structure of alien origin, pulsating with an otherworldly glow. The final guard details were stationed here, and they put up a fierce fight. Laser bolts cut through the air, casting long eerie shadows. The echoing booms of their weapons, the screams, and the sharp smell of ozone filled the massive room. Suddenly, a chilling voice resonated through the base's intercoms, its tone cold and threatening. "Commander, you and your friends will die here!" A threat from the faction leader herself, as recognized by Dr. M'dious. It was a disconcerting reminder that their mission was far from over. The fight raged on, intense and deadly, the team knew they were at the very heart of the enemy's operation. And they were committed to putting an end to it. The ferocity of the conflict heightened as the leader of the faction finally appeared. She was a lithe figure, her small stature in stark contrast to the massive auto blaster cannon she wielded with surprising ease. Her menacing silhouette cut a deadly figure against the ominous light cast by the monolithic device. McKinley, known for his unshakeable demeanor, was visibly taken aback. He marveled at the sight, murmuring, "Well, I'll be... didn't see that comin'." The leader's demonstration of power and control over such a formidable weapon was indeed an unexpected and intimidating sight. Despite the looming threat, the team's resolve hardened. They had come too far to be deterred now. The battle roared on, reaching a crescendo as the leader joined the fray. The fate of the Erisian space and the success of their mission hung in the balance. Moore, who during this time had been hanging back managing to down many of the faction's soldiers spotted the leader out in the open. Putting the leader in her sights she exhaled all her breath and fired. The round piercing the leader's upper chest. Moore's precise shot caught the faction leader off guard. She fell to the ground, her imposing weapon slipping from her grasp to land with a thud on the ground. The echoes of the last gunshots dwindled into silence as the rest of the team emerged from their cover. The smell of smoke and cordite hung heavily in the air. A settling dust filled the room, casting the scene in an eerie, subdued light. The imposing figure of the monolith towered at the center of the chaos, untouched and eerily quiet. Its existence, however, served as a reminder of the danger it could potentially unleash, heightening the team's awareness as they cautiously approached the device. "We did it," Reyes breathed out, his voice echoing slightly in the large chamber. Yet his gaze remained fixed on the monolith, a grim reminder of the mission's true purpose. Their struggle was far from over; the device needed to be secured, and the consequences of its activation had to be understood and contained. But for the moment, they could take a small victory in overcoming the immediate threat. "Moore, secure the device" the commander ordered, he then turned to the Dr. M'dious. "Your data suggested it was handheld device what is thi..." Suddenly the device activated and began to pull Moore upwards her body levitating off the ground. As Moore floated there in the brilliant light, the room around her seemed to bend and twist, giving the eerie impression that reality was warping. Reyes, Mckinley, and Dr. M'dious could only look on in shock.

"M-Moore!" Reyes stammered, "Hang on!"

Reyes darted towards Moore's levitating body attempting to tackle her off the device. Lunging towards Moore, the force from the monolith sucked him in, its grip tightening like an unseen hand. Moore dropped back to the ground as Reyes was pulled towards the monolith. The commander's eyes then rolled into the back of his head, floating motionless.

"Commander!" Mckinley yelled, starting towards him but Dr. M'dious held him back, her eyes wide with fear and awe as they watched the spectacle unfolding.

As Reyes was ensnared by the monolith's power, his mind was flooded with a vision. His world turned black, save for a series of images that flickered like a film reel. He saw a future, devastated and torn. Planet after planet within the Federation lay in ruins, their cities aflame, their people scattered or dead. He saw fleets of ships unlike any he'd ever seen before. They had a dark, mechanical aesthetic - no soft organic lines or human warmth. The ships pulsed with an eerie red glow, and they swarmed through space like a horde of cosmic locusts. The vision shifted, revealing the entities controlling these vessels. They were not organic beings as he'd seen before, but beings of metal and electricity, their forms alien and horrifying. Cold and emotionless, they tore through civilizations, their single-minded purpose clear: complete annihilation. The hue of purple and green energy swirled around Reyes, an ethereal cocoon that seemed to pulse with the rhythm of the monolith. Then, with a blinding flash of light that filled the room, Reyes was thrust away from the monolith, skidding across the floor, motionless. As Reyes lay motionless on the ground, the intensity of the vision fading from his mind, his team and Dr. M'dious rushed to his side. The doctor, her medical instincts kicking in, quickly checked for a pulse. It was there - weak, but steady.

"Commander Reyes is alive," Dr. M'dious announced, her voice carrying a note of relief.

McKinley and Moore exchanged a glance. They were hardened soldiers, used to the unpredictability and danger of their missions, but seeing their commander in this state was a shock. It was a reminder of how dire their situation truly was.

McKinley was the first to move, radioing the ship. "Syv, we need immediate extraction. Commander's down."

In the aftermath of the battle, the team prepared for a swift retreat, with their commander's unconscious form in tow. Their mission had taken a dire turn, unknown to them the entire galaxy was at stake.

CHAPTER 11

Safely back on the ship now, on the medical bed lay Commander Reyes, he began to stir. His crew now by his side, watching his movements. Dr. M'dious was reviewing his vitals and scanning his brain functions. The commander now moving more struggled to sit up right, the doctor assisted him up. He looked around, out the ship's window the vast expanse of space could be seen, waves of energy rushing over the window as the ship's shields protected them from the outside.
"Wha...What happened?" Reyes strained.
Dr. M'dious answered in her calm and collected tone, "Commander, you experienced a severe psychic trauma. The monolith... it reacted to your touch, and you lost consciousness." Syv, who was standing by the foot of his bed, added, "We've already left the Orion Nebula Commander. We on our way back to Earth as we speak."
Reyes squinted his eyes, trying to piece together the fragments of the horrifying vision he'd seen. "I... I saw... something," he finally muttered, his voice barely above a whisper.
The room fell silent as everyone turned their attention to him. "What did you see, Reyes?" Moore finally broke the silence, her voice laced with worry.
Reyes paused for a moment, recalling the horrific images that still lingered in his mind. "I saw... a vision. A future... our future,

it wasn't pretty," he began, his gaze focused on nothing in particular as he recounted the horrifying prophecy. "In my vision, there were these other beings... Not organic... And they were destructive, hostile, evil." His words were met with shared glances of concern among his team.

Dr. M'dious interjected, "It's possible the monolith triggered a deep psychic episode. Your brain may have created those images."

Reyes shook his head, certain of the reality of his vision. "No," he countered, his gaze distant yet determined. "It felt too real, too... malevolent. There were beings, not organic ones. Their malevolence... I could feel it. It was palpable, insidious."

"Could it be an insight into an impending threat?" Mckinley suggested, his words trailing off into the silence of the room.

Reyes slowly nodded. "That's what I fear, Mckinley. That's what I fear. And we must be ready."

"Commander." Moore interjected. "If what you say is true, then the Federation Council will need to hear your words. They will have to understand you commander."

Dr. M'dious nodded, adding her support to Moore's words. "Commander, I've studied ancient relics and their energy signatures for years, but what you've described... this is beyond anything I've ever encountered. The entire galaxy may be at stake here. You have witnessed it firsthand, and your words carry weight as a decorated officer of the Federation."

Reyes sat on the edge of the bed, his gaze distant as he pondered the gravity of the situation. His crew, and even Dr. M'dious, looked at him with concern and anticipation. Finally, he stood up with determination.

"You're right," he said, his voice resonating with the authority and resolve that had made him a respected leader. "This is bigger than us. We need to warn the Federation and rally every ally we can find. This may be the greatest threat we have ever faced."

He turned to Syv, who had remained silent but was clearly eager to help. "Syv, set a course for the Federation Council at the highest speed possible. Moore, get all the data and information we have on this. We'll need every bit of it." "And Dr. M'dious," Reyes continued, turning to the Erisian scientist, "I need you to gather everything you know about the monolith, its history, and any related legends or facts. It may help us understand what we're up against." The room was alive with energy as everyone sprang into action. In mere hours, they were standing before the Federation Council, a vast chamber filled with representatives from countless worlds. The seriousness of the situation had allowed for an emergency session to be called. Commander Reyes stood tall before them and began to speak. His words were clear and his presence commanding as he recounted his vision, the monolith, and the looming threat that was unlike anything the galaxy had faced before.

◆ ◆ ◆

Back on Earth, Commander Reyes and his team stood once again before the council members. The room was thick with tension as Reyes finished recounting his story. Their faces were unreadable, etched with years of diplomatic discipline. Admiral Lawson, the Fleet Commander of the Federation, was the first to break the silence. "Commander Reyes, we respect you as a dedicated officer of the Federation. But what you're suggesting... it's nothing short of fantastical."
Vice Admiral Nia Patel, the Logistical Commander, chimed in, her icy eyes examining Reyes. "We are a council of facts, Commander. And facts do not include prophecies and visions, no matter how vividly experienced."
General Alfonso Diaz, the Administrative Commander, weighed in with a calm but firm voice, "Commander, we operate on tangible intelligence and strategic evaluation, not on dreams

and visions."

Finally, General Amelia Warner, Ground Commander of the Federation forces, offered her perspective. Her battle-hardened face betrayed no emotion as she said, "In the world we live in, we cannot act on such unsubstantiated threats."

The dismissal was clear. They were not going to act on his words, not without proof. But Reyes wasn't ready to back down. "I assure you, I'm not just seeing visions. There is something coming, and if we're not prepared, we won't stand a chance." Admiral Lawson gave a final nod, indicating the end of the discussion. "We appreciate your concern, Commander Reyes. But without concrete evidence, the council cannot and will not act on prophetic warnings." As the team left the council chambers, a heavy sense of dread washed over them. They knew the truth, but without the council's support, they were on their own. Yet, Reyes was not about to give up. Whatever it took, he would find a way to make the galaxy ready for what was coming.

Outside the council chambers, in the crisp air of Earth's midday, the tension among the team was palpable. Yet, Mckinley, always the one to lighten the mood, attempted to crack a joke. "Well, seems like we're the galaxy's unwanted stepchildren now, eh?" He chuckled, looking around at his crewmates, expecting them to join in.

However, Reyes was in no mood for humor. His stern gaze landed on Mckinley, his voice graver than ever. "This is no time for levity, Mckinley. We're on to something monumental here. Something that could change everything we know about our place in the universe."

Mckinley fell silent, nodding in understanding. Reyes' determination was infectious. Despite the council's dismissal, they all knew they would follow their Commander into the ends of the universe if that's what it took. Because they trusted him. Because he was right. And because they were a team, regardless of who chose to stand with them or against them. Moore chimed in, attempting to dissolve the tension. Her words were softer, a friendly chide layered with underlying respect for both Reyes and Mckinley. "Come on, Commander, don't be so hard on the big guy," she said, giving Mckinley a supportive nod. Her eyes then shifted to Reyes, a look of unwavering trust reflecting in them.

"We've faced insurmountable problems before, haven't we, Commander?" she continued, a ghost of a smile dancing on her lips, "This time won't be any different. We can do it... we will do it."

There was something about Moore's faith in them that invigorated the crew, a spark of hope that pushed the cloud of dismissal away. They knew the journey ahead wouldn't be easy, but with Reyes leading them and their collective strength to rely on, they were ready to face whatever the universe had in store for them.

Reyes nodded, giving Moore a grudging smile. "You're right, Moore," he conceded, "We are going to need friends, a lot of them. And allies." He paused, running a hand through his hair. His next words came out heavy, a mixture of determination and concern.

"We need to find Stevens too. That man always seems to be one step ahead, seems like when something big is going down he's there. Last we know, he was seen on Lysithea."

His eyes met each of his crew, a silent vow passing between them. "There must be something, or someone there, that can give us a lead to pick up his trail," he continued, "We can't let him slip away this time." The consensus was clear amongst them. Their next destination was set: Lysithea. As the crew walked away from the Council Chamber, they were ready to face the next phase of their mission, even if it meant standing against the entire universe.

◆ ◆ ◆

Back on Lysithea, they came across an unusual scene at the outskirts of the town. A group of mercenaries had gathered, their grim expressions creating a tense atmosphere. Dr. M'dious recognized the insignia of several rival factions among them - the Red Serpents, the Obsidian Hawks, the Azure Typhoons. These groups had been at each other's throats for years. Their presence together was alarming.

"Seeing them united like this... It's clear they all have a common enemy," the doctor murmured, surveying the scene. Reyes scanned the crowd, his ears perked at the sound of hushed conversations. He strained to make out the words, and his eyes widened as he caught the mention of a certain name. A hushed whisper of a name seemed to circulate among the group - "Auriel". A man known for his seemingly supernatural ability to singlehandedly face down armies of mercenaries. The very mention of the name caused a ripple of tension to spread through the crowd.

"Doctor," Reyes said, turning to M'dious, "Have you ever heard of this Auriel?"

M'dious looked thoughtful for a moment before shaking her head. "The name doesn't ring a bell. But it seems this individual has the mercenaries spooked."

Reyes frowned, thoughtful. "We need to find out more about this Auriel. He might be connected to Stevens... or even the unknown threat we're facing." He glanced back at the assembled mercenaries, a determined look in his eyes. "Let's see what we can find out." The Red Serpent mercenary leaned closer, lowering his voice to a gruff whisper as he spoke. "Listen up, this ain't a simple job. You've got to distract an individual named Auriel."

He activated a small handheld device, projecting a holographic image into the air between them. The image showed a figure, distinctively armored and unmistakably non-human, an imposing Veloran, a bipedal bird-like species known for their armor-like skin and fearsome combat abilities.

"Your job," he explained, his tone as cold as steel, "is to get his attention. Keep him busy. You'll be the distraction."

He continued, "Once you've got him focused on you, we'll come in and finish the job. You're the fodder, we're the damage dealers."

Reyes examined the image, meeting the eyes of the armored Veloran, a spark of determination igniting within him. This could be their best chance to locate Stevens and get closer to understanding the threat they faced.

"Alright," he said, looking back at the Red Serpent mercenary, his gaze steady and unwavering. "We're in."

"Good" as the mercenary gestured over his shoulder, "There's a shuttle parked nearby. You can't miss it, got our logo on it." He pulled a couple of cards from his pocket and handed them over to Reyes. "Show these to the pilot. He'll let you on and you'll be on your way."

His expression hardened as he leaned in closer, "Just know this... Auriel, he's tough. Already killed two of my commanders." He thumped his chest with a gloved fist, "But he won't kill the next one. Me." His voice was a gravelly growl, full of confidence and anticipation.

"We've finally got the bastard cornered. He won't last much longer. That's where you four come in." The mercenary smirked, clearly believing in their impending success.

"Now get out of here," he finished, turning his back on them, and walking away, leaving Reyes and his crew with the task of facing the notorious Veloran. The path ahead was uncertain, but their resolve was unyielding. They were prepared to face whatever lay in store for them.

Moore, looking skeptical, turned to Reyes. "Are we really going to help these psychos?" she asked, her voice dripping with disbelief.

Reyes, ever the stoic leader, simply nodded, his gaze locked onto the shuttle the mercenary had pointed out. "We're not helping them, Moore," he reassured her. "We're going in to disrupt their plans, find this Auriel. If what the merc said is true, then Auriel could be a powerful ally in the battles to come."

His words hung in the air as the crew stood in silence, contemplating their next move. They were walking into the lion's den, but if it meant getting the upper hand in the looming conflict, they were ready to face the challenge. As the sun set on Lysithea, they embarked on their new mission, unaware of the trials that lay ahead. The game was afoot, and only time would tell who would emerge as the victor.

CHAPTER 12

Upon disembarking from the shuttle, the crew found themselves in a once vibrant, now abandoned town. It served as a makeshift staging ground for the mercenaries. Among the usual rundown and weathered buildings, an enormous robot mech stood out, its blue and orange armor indicative of the Azure Typhoons' ownership. The hulking figure of the mech was marred with the evidence of recent conflict; it was riddled with holes burned through its armor, a tangible testament to its last engagement. Near the mechanical giant, a mechanic could be seen toiling, his body slick with sweat under the harsh sun. A burning cigarette hung loosely from his lips as he leaned against a stool, taking a much-needed break from his daunting task. The mechanic's worn-out state was reflective of the atmosphere that hung heavily over the town. The mercs had taken quite a beating, but they were far from out. Their grim determination could be felt in the very air, a tangible force against the looming threat of Auriel.

Reyes glanced at his crew, exchanging knowing looks. This was going to be a tough mission. But then again, they had faced tougher odds before. With determination setting in, they headed deeper into the staging ground, ready to face what awaited them. As the crew approached the mechanic, he took notice of them, his eyes narrowing in suspicion. "What do you four dipshits want?" he asked gruffly, a scowl marring his greasy face. "Never seen real work before?"

Reyes, unflappable as always, retorted with a smirk, "Oh, we've seen work, alright. Just not someone turning a wreck into a bigger wreck."

The mechanic's face flushed at Reyes' words, his scowl deepening. But before he could retort, McKinley's booming laugh echoed through the open space. The sight of the mechanic sputtering, caught between anger and embarrassment, was too much for the burly soldier. He slapped his knee, his laughter only growing louder.

Even in the midst of their dangerous mission, the crew found room for levity. It was a welcome distraction from the grim task that lay ahead. The mechanic's face turned a shade of red akin to the armor of the Red Serpent mercs as he spat out, "Watch it! Around here, lives are cheap, and you lot are replaceable. Veerry replaceable, if you catch my drift."

In a blink, Reyes closed the distance and grabbed the mechanic, efficiently putting him into a headlock. A swift chop to the neck and the mechanic was down, unconscious. Moore was already on the mech, her fingers flying over its control panel. The others took up defensive positions, watching for any mercs who might have been alerted by the commotion.

"What you doing there, Moore?" Mckinley asked, peeking over her shoulder.

"I'm altering the targeting parameters of this mech. The moment it activates, it's going to wreak havoc on these mercs," she said, her voice filled with grim determination.

"Bloody 'ell, gotta make sure that thing don't turn us into Swiss cheese, love" Mckinley muttered.

As they wrapped up, they heard a voice crackling over the communication channel of the downed mechanic. "Report in! We're moving on Auriel's position in five."

Reyes signaled to his team. "Time to move. Moore, initiate the mech when we reach a safe distance. We use the chaos to our advantage." They moved quickly through the decaying buildings of the abandoned town, sticking to the shadows. When they were well away from the mech, Moore pressed a button on a remote.

A series of explosions echoed in the distance as the reprogrammed mech opened fire. The comm channel was flooded with shouts and the clattering noise of return fire.

"This is it," Reyes whispered. "Let's find Auriel and see what side of this fight he's really on."

Chaos reigned in the streets as the reprogrammed mech lumbered around, its weapons firing indiscriminately at the mercs. The air was filled with the sounds of gunfire, screams, and explosions. Mercs were darting back and forth, some trying to retaliate against the rogue mech, others just trying to find cover. Reyes and his crew were swift and silent, darting through narrow alleys and across shadowy streets, staying low and out of sight. A bullet zipped past, close enough to send shivers down their spines, but they pressed on, undeterred. Suddenly, Reyes held up his hand, signaling the team to stop. He pointed at a tall building in the center of the town. Even amidst the chaos, a lone figure could be seen occasionally peeking out from the rooftop to take shots at the mercs below.

"That's him, that's Auriel. Let's go," Reyes said, his voice barely above a whisper but filled with certainty.

The team nodded, sharing a quick, determined glance before dashing off toward the building, their every step echoing the rhythm of their throbbing hearts. The looming confrontation with the notorious Auriel was only moments away. The team moved as one, their training and years of experience in high-stakes missions evident in the synchronicity of their movements. They navigated through the winding backstreets, edging closer to the building where Auriel was perched. The stench of gunpowder and blood hung heavy in the air, a grim testament to the fierce battle that had just taken place. At the rear of the building, they found a narrow staircase spiraling upwards. One by one, they ascended, their boots tapping lightly against the cold, metal steps. The atmosphere was tense, the only sounds being their controlled breathing and the distant echoes of Auriel's relentless onslaught against the mercs. As they neared the rooftop, they slowed their pace, moving with extreme caution. They knew well the reputation that preceded Auriel, and they were prepared to handle anything they might throw their way. Reyes signaled for his team to hold their positions at the top of the stairs while he moved forward to engage Auriel. Their mission was clear - find Auriel, understand his motives, and if possible, convince them to join their cause. As Reyes stepped onto the rooftop, he knew that the next few moments could very well decide the fate of the galaxy. Auriel was aiming down the sights into the street when Reyes' team reached them. Realizing their presence, the armored Veloran cracked a half-smile. "Ah, Eli Reyes, good you finally showed up," they quipped, not taking their gaze off her scope. "Thought I was going to have to kill all these bastards myself."

A flicker of recognition passed through Reyes' eyes, and he lowered his weapon. "Vela?" he called out, using the real name of his old friend, not the infamous moniker they went by now.

The Veloran turned to face him, her eyes softening at the familiar voice. "The very same," she replied with a faint smile, a rare sight for anyone who knew Auriel the mercenary. "It's been a while, Eli. To what do I owe the pleasure?" Her voice was laced with curiosity and a hint of wariness, knowing full well that Reyes would not seek her out without a good reason. Removing her helmet, Vela's face came into view. She looked worn and weary, the relentless onslaught clearly taking its toll. Her deep blue eyes, a characteristic feature of the Veloran species, showed a fatigue that even her strong demeanor couldn't mask. "I won't lie, Eli, I was running on fumes here," she admitted, her voice husky with exhaustion.

Reyes looked at her with concern, but quickly composed himself, responding to her previous question. "We're looking for Lynn Stevens. The bastard that everyone thought was dead."

Vela's tired eyes narrowed at the mention of the name. "Stevens?" she asked, a hint of surprise in her tone.

Reyes nodded. "Turns out he doesn't much care for our world. Has intentions of destroying it."

Vela let out a dry chuckle. "Yeah, sounds like him alright. If anyone were to bear a grudge that long, it'd be him." The graveness of the situation was not lost on her, but years of battlefield humor had taught her to laugh, even in the face of imminent danger. "So, what's the plan, Eli?" she asked, looking at her old friend, ready to follow his lead. "Track the son of a bitch down," Reyes said, an unwavering determination in his voice, "Then stop whatever he's got planned."

Vela nodded, her feathered head making a slight rustling sound. "Sounds like a plan. But we've got a little problem to deal with first. These mercs - in case you hadn't noticed - they want me dead. But we're going to turn the tables on them, right cap?"

Reyes agreed, a faint smile playing on his lips at her term of familiarity. "Just like old times then. And it's 'Commander' now, Vela."

With a teasing sparkle in her eyes, Vela raised her hands in a mock surrender, her armored fingers catching the faint glow of the setting sun. "Oh ho, I'm sorry, 'Commander'," she joked, a smirk forming on her beak-like mouth, further lightening the grim atmosphere. Despite the dire circumstances, their bond and shared past brought a sense of camaraderie that lent them strength in this battle. They were ready for what lay ahead. With a determined look on his face, Commander Reyes began pointing out positions to his team. "Moore, take point," he said, gesturing to a spot beside Vela. "Help Vela with her sniping skills."

Next, he turned to McKinley, his hand directing towards the staircase. "McKinley, guard the front door. Make sure those mercs regret even thinking about trying to knock."

His eyes then landed on Dr. M'dious. "Doctor, hang back. If your psionic powers can be of any use in a battle, I suggest you use them."

Lastly, he turned to Vela, giving her a nod of approval. "Vela, just keep doing what you're doing, it seems to be working."

He finished with a decisive air about him, a leader inspiring confidence in his team. "Let's go to work."

With their orders in hand, the team sprang into action, ready to take on the waves of mercenaries that dared to cross their path.

◆ ◆ ◆

The first wave of mercenaries came on, a sea of hardened faces beneath armored helmets. They were the light infantry, cannon fodder meant to test the team's defenses. But the team was ready, their focus unwavering as they prepared to meet the assault. Moore and Vela worked in perfect sync, their sniper shots echoing through the otherwise quiet battlefield, picking off mercenaries one by one. Their aim was deadly accurate, each bullet finding its mark in the oncoming wave of enemies. Downstairs, McKinley stood firm, his weapon of choice a high-energy plasma blaster. Each time the front door shuddered under the weight of a merc trying to force entry, he was there to repel them, sending a powerful blast of energy that knocked them off their feet. From the back, Dr. M'dious aided with her Psionic Powers, creating barriers to protect her teammates, and throwing mercenaries off balance with her mind. Her presence was a constant reassurance, her abilities providing an edge that helped even the odds. And in the midst of it all was Commander Reyes, directing his team, his focus split between the immediate threats and the next wave of mercs preparing to launch their assault. Bombs exploded, laser beams cut through the air, and kinetic weapons sent shockwaves through the ground, but the team held their ground. The battle raged on, a testament to the strength and determination of Reyes' team. But this was just the beginning. The mercenaries were far from defeated, and the fight was far from over. The few left fighting in the streets turned and retreated back across their barriers. Multitude of dead Mercs lined the streets and with that the first wave been repelled.

"Status report," Reyes called out, his voice echoing over the sounds of the dying battle.

From her vantage point, Moore was the first to respond. "Clear on my end, Commander. Plenty of targets down."

"Same here," Dr. M'dious chimed in. Her voice was slightly breathless, the physical toll of using her Psionic Powers evident. "No injuries on our side."

From the ground level, Mckinley's voice sounded a bit too cheerful. "Holding the front door just fine, Commander. Made a nice pile of would-be intruders. It's almost like they don't like being greeted with plasma bolts."

Finally, Vela's voice crackled through the comms. "Sniping duty's a breeze with Moore. She's got quite an aim. Plenty of reds down."

Reyes allowed himself a small grin at Mckinley's quip. The team was holding up well, but they needed to prepare for the next wave. "Good job, everyone. Stay sharp. This is far from over."

Mckinley chimed back in, "Commander, I'm going to lay a few booby traps down on the streets. Have Moore and Vela on overwatch for me, would ya? When these Mercs come through, it's gonna be one cock-up on their end."

Reyes confirmed his intentions but told him to make it fast. "Ladies," speaking to Moore and Vela, "keep an eye on our big brute friend, would ya?"

"You got it, Commander!" Moore replied with a smirk, adjusting her scope.

Vela simply nodded, her keen eyes scanning the surroundings.

As Mckinley dashed across the battlefield, dodging bullets, and laying down traps, Moore and Vela provided covering fire, picking off any mercs that got too close to Mckinley. The air was thick with smoke and the scent of charred metal as the trio worked in tandem. The doctor, meanwhile, was focusing her psionic powers to create barriers and deflect projectiles. It was a sight to behold; the raw energy emanating from her seemed almost tangible. As the second wave of mercs charged forward, one of Mckinley's traps detonated, wiping out an entire squad. The Mercs had begun to realize they were outmatched, as chaos and disarray spread through their ranks.

Reyes took advantage of this moment, giving the order, "Push forward! We have them on the back foot!"

What followed was a relentless charge as the team, along with Vela, cut through the mercs like a scythe through wheat. After what seemed like an eternity, the last of the Mercs fell. The team was victorious, but at a heavy cost. The area was devastated, and the members were drained and injured. However, they had bought themselves some precious time.

Reyes turned to Vela, "Now that this is done, we need to find Stevens."

Vela looked back at him with a determined glare. "Lead the way, Commander."

They gathered their gear and set off, knowing that this was just the first hurdle in a mission that could determine the fate of the galaxy.

Reyes perched himself on top of a barrier a single leg dangling as he grabbed his communication device. "Governor Illiana, can you hear me, this is Commander Reyes, please respond."

"Commander Reyes," Illiana's voice crackled through the comm, "Good to hear from you. Are you and the team alright, heard you went after Auriel."

"We've seen better days, Illiana," Reyes replied, his tone conveying the severity of the situation. "We're going to need extraction, and fast. And while you're at it, prepare the medical team. We have wounded. Also, get the morgue ready. This place... it's a massacre."

The line went silent for a moment before Illiana responded. "Understood, Commander. I'll dispatch a recovery team immediately. Stay safe and try to keep out of trouble until they arrive."

Reyes couldn't help but chuckle, "No promises, Illiana. Reyes out." He cut the connection and turned back to his team, a look of determination in his eyes.

Healing and recovery awaited them back on the ship, but so did the next steps of their mission. The search for Stevens and his ominous plans was far from over. But for now, they had a moment to breathe. A moment to regroup.

Awaiting their extraction, they moved by through the city a torn apart by the massive battle. Walking through the street Reyes decided to break the silence

"Auriel, huh?" Reyes looked at Vela, a playful smirk on his face. "What, are you some divine creature now? Come to smite us mere mortals?"

Vela laughed, her laughter a refreshing sound amidst the grim aftermath of the battle. "Well, someone's got to keep you all in line. Might as well be a divine creature."

As her laughter subsided, McKinley chimed in, a grin broad on his face. "Haha, I like this one, Commander," he said, giving Vela an approving nod. "She reminds me of me self."

Reyes couldn't help but chuckle at the camaraderie forming amidst the harsh reality of their mission. Despite the gravity of their situation, moments like these served as a much-needed reminder of the bond that tied them all together, a bond that would hold them strong in the face of whatever awaited them next.

The laughter in the air faded as Vela spoke again, her tone shifting to a more serious one. "Actually, the mercs named me that," she explained, her icy gaze meeting Reyes' eyes. "Quite impressive, really. I didn't think those jerks had more than two brain cells clicking around up there." The low hum of engines echoed overhead, drawing their eyes skyward. Once a distant speck, grew larger as it rapidly approached their position.

"Looks like our ride," Reyes remarked, his eyes tracking the shuttle as it prepared to descend. "Double time, everyone. I don't want to stay here any longer than we need to."

The team, despite their exhaustion, responded instantly, picking up the pace. They moved as one, their footsteps falling in a synchronized rhythm that cut through the stillness of the devastated city. The shuttle touched down ahead of them, its rear hatch opening to reveal a welcoming, albeit temporary, haven. Their task was far from over, but for now, they would have a moment's respite. The extraction shuttle, a symbol of their successful mission, waited to ferry them away from the war-torn cityscape and toward their next challenge.

CHAPTER 13

As Reyes sat in the crew hall of the Bushido, he couldn't help but feel a sense of pride swelling within him. His team - Moore, McKinley, Dr. M'dious, and now Vela - had grown and come together in ways he could never have anticipated. Moore, always the tech specialist, was completely engrossed in her scanner device, her fingers flying over the controls as she processed data at a speed that left most people dizzy. McKinley, the lovable brute, was half-sunk into a bottle of whiskey, his eyes slightly glassy but his spirits high. Dr. M'dious, the Erisian with an uncanny knack for psionic powers, was silently honing her skills, a faint aura of energy flickering around her. Vela, the fierce Veloran sniper they'd recently acquired, was methodically polishing her rifle, her movements a ballet of deadly precision. Despite the camaraderie and the victories, a sense of urgency still hung in the air. They were no closer to figuring out what Lynn Stevens was planning and how to stop it. The man owed Reyes a ship, a score he was determined to settle. But more than that, there was a galactic threat looming over them. The clock was ticking, and time was a luxury they couldn't afford. Reyes took a deep breath, letting the worries of their mission fill his lungs before he exhaled them out, replacing them with resolve. His gaze moved from one crew member to the next, a silent vow passing between them. They had faced insurmountable odds before, and they would do so again. After all, they were not just a crew. They were a family. And they would face the universe's challenges together.

"Commander Reyes, this is Governor Illiana, I think I have something you might be interested in," Illiana's voice came through the communication device, pulling Reyes from his reverie. Reyes sat up straighter in his seat, his gaze sharpening as he listened. "Go ahead, Illiana. I'm listening," he responded, his tone clipped and focused. There was a brief pause on the other end of the line before Illiana continued. "My intelligence network managed to pick up a certain individual during a routine sweep. He's been rather... talkative," she said, her tone betraying her satisfaction. Reyes' heart started to beat faster in his chest. "What does this have to do with Lynn Stevens?" he asked, keeping his tone steady. Another pause on Illiana's end before she finally dropped the bombshell. "This individual claims to have information on Stevens. According to him, he's seen Stevens very recently." Reyes felt a surge of adrenaline at Illiana's words. It was the first substantial lead they had on Stevens in what felt like an eternity. "I'm on my way," he replied, ending the call as he sprung up from his seat. The rest of the crew looked up in alarm as he moved quickly towards the exit. "We've got a lead on Stevens," he told them, his tone hard and his eyes focused. "Gear up. We're heading out."

◆ ◆ ◆

Navigating through the labyrinth of underground passages beneath Lysithea, Governor Illiana guided Commander Reyes, Moore, and McKinley to a secured holding area. Their captive was restrained, back against a sturdy metal pole, a mix of fear and surprise washing over his face when his eyes landed on Reyes. His features were gaunt, his eyes hollow. He wore a dirty, disheveled uniform bearing a sigil that Reyes recognized - a symbol often associated with Lynn Stevens' allies. The governor moved to stand next to Reyes, her voice barely a whisper as she nodded towards the captive. "Do what you must, Commander," she said. Her gaze never wavered from the prisoner as she signaled her guards to exit the room. With a nod to Reyes, she turned on her heel and left, the heavy door closing behind her with an ominous thud. The room fell into silence, the air thick with tension. Reyes, his face set in a hardened mask, stepped forward to begin the interrogation. Now alone with their captive, they hoped to extract crucial information that could help them stop Stevens. Reyes approached the prisoner with a hardened look in his eyes. He sized up the captive, gauging his reaction before finally speaking. "You know who I am," he said, his tone steady. "You know why I'm here." The prisoner sneered, a glimmer of defiance in his eyes. "Reyes," he spat out. "I wondered when you'd come sniffing around." "Cut the crap," Mckinley chimed in, crossing his arms over his chest. "We're here for one reason, and it ain't to exchange pleasantries." Ignoring the comment, Reyes leaned in closer, his voice dropping to a menacing whisper. "We're here for information on Stevens. You're going to tell us everything." The captive smirked, meeting Reyes' gaze with a defiant one of his own. "And what makes you think I'd do that?" "Because," Reyes said, standing upright and crossing his arms, "You have a choice. Help us, and you might live to see another day. Refuse, and you'll wish you hadn't." In the tense silence that followed, Moore moved to stand next to Reyes, her eyes never leaving the captive. It was clear she was ready to back up Reyes' words with action if necessary. "We don't have time for games," Reyes added, his gaze locked onto the prisoner. "So I'll ask again: What do you know about Lynn Stevens?" The prisoner smirked, a mirthless laugh escaping his lips. "You think you can intimidate me, Reyes?" he asked, his voice laced with defiance. "I've faced worse than you." "Is that so?" Reyes asked, his voice chillingly calm. "I guess we'll see about that." Without another word, Reyes signaled to Moore. She approached the prisoner, her hands sparking with electrical energy. "You may have faced worse," she said, "but I doubt you've faced anything like this." Moore pressed her hands against the captive, letting a controlled surge of energy course through him. The captive gritted his teeth, his body writhing against the bindings as pain seared through him. Yet, he refused to break, his smirk transforming into a defiant sneer. Mckinley stepped forward, cracking his knuckles. "Let me have a go at em," he said, a twisted grin on his face. The room echoed with the sounds of Mckinley's methodical, painful persuasion. They took turns, each bringing their own brand of persuasion to bear. Hours turned into what seemed like days. However, their captive proved more stubborn than they had anticipated. His defiance didn't waver, even under the intense pain. Finally, Reyes called a halt, staring down at the battered, but unbroken prisoner. The silence in the room was heavy, filled with the unspoken acknowledgement that they were at an impasse. Then Reyes did something unexpected. He knelt down to the prisoner's level, staring him directly in the eyes. "Alright," he said, his voice quiet but firm. "We'll do this your way. No more pain. Just a simple question: Why? Why protect a man like Stevens?" The room held its breath, waiting for the prisoner's response. "Mars, Commander," the captive's voice lowered, his gaze turning deadly serious. "That's the key. That's where the Ascendancy will begin. That's where our legions are gathering." "Legions?" Reyes' voice was a mere whisper. His mind was trying to process the information, but it was difficult. The idea of an army of droids was horrifying enough, but the captive's next words chilled him to the bone. "People, Commander," the captive said, a twisted smile playing on his lips. "Willing participants. They've given their bodies, their very essence, over to become part of the army.

Humans, aliens, doesn't matter. They've seen the truth. The Ascendancy... it's inevitable." Reyes felt a knot form in his stomach. The scale of what he was hearing was staggering. A force of such magnitude could potentially overrun the Federation. "Mars," he repeated to himself, thinking of the red planet. The captive's words echoed in his mind. 'Legions. Droids. Ascendancy.' A shiver ran down his spine. This was bigger than he thought, much bigger. They needed to act, and they needed to do so quickly. Lynn Stevens and his Ascendancy needed to be stopped. The man's fervor seemed to consume him, his body thrashing wildly against the restraints. Spittle flew from his lips as he ranted about the Ascendancy, his eyes wide and filled with an unsettling fanaticism. His words became disjointed, his sentences less coherent as he spiraled further into madness. "The Ascendancy! The Ascendancy! Salvation!" he cried, his voice growing hoarse from the strain. His movements became more erratic, the bindings creaking under the force. Suddenly, he went still, his head lolling forward onto his chest. His final breath was a ragged whisper, "Salvation... Ascendancy..." And with that, he fell silent, succumbing to the profound trauma his body and mind had endured. The room was once again filled with an eerie silence, the prisoner's maniacal rants no longer echoing off the cold, stone walls. Reyes, Moore, and McKinley exchanged concerned looks. This was a level of fanaticism they hadn't anticipated, and it left them all with a deep sense of unease. Their mission had just become a lot more complicated. Reyes and his companions emerged from the underground base, with Illiana waiting outside. "Find what you were looking for, Commander?" she asked, her voice reflecting a mixture of concern and curiosity. Reyes's face was stern. "Partly," he replied. "But what we found is far more disturbing than what we imagined." Illiana arched an eyebrow. "What do you mean?" "Mars," Reyes began, "it seems to be some kind of focal point for whatever Stevens is planning. And there's an army... People are willingly converting themselves into droids for him. They believe in some kind of higher power and that Stevens is the one to lead them to salvation." Illiana's face paled. "This is far worse than we anticipated. An army of fanatics, hell-bent on some twisted form of salvation." "Yes," Reyes agreed. "And there's something else, the man we interrogated..." He looked over to Moore and McKinley, who both had grim expressions. "He was not sane. Something had driven him to madness. He mentioned visions and higher powers." "Sounds like a cult," McKinley chimed in. "What's the plan, Commander?" Moore asked, ever the professional. Reyes took a deep breath. "First, we need to inform the Federation Council about what we've uncovered. And second, we need to find out more about what's happening on Mars. If that's where Stevens is, that's where we need to be." Illiana placed her hand on Reyes' shoulder. "You have Lysithea's support, Commander. Whatever resources you need, they're yours." "Thank you, Governor," Reyes nodded. They made their way back to the shuttle to return to the Bushido. As they boarded, Reyes looked back at Lysithea. The stakes had been raised, and now more than ever, they needed to put an end to Stevens' mad plans before it was too late.

CHAPTER 14

Back on the Bushido, Commander Reyes was pacing back and forth, trying to make a plan of action. He stopped and turned to Syv who was sitting at the controls of the ship.

"Syv" the commander called out.

Syv swiveling in the pilot's seat answered "Yes, commander?"

"Do know anyone or anything that could be willing to join our cause?" he paused and moved to an outer window peering out. "We need all the help we can get, I fear our current crew isn't quite enough."

"On my recent data collection, I identified four individuals that might be inclined to join our cause, Commander," said Syv, in his robotic speech pattern.

"Go on, Syv," Reyes encouraged.

"First, there is Rak'thor Kresh, a Drakkan, known for his strength and combat skills. He was a former warlord but was dethroned and is seeking revenge. His motivation aligns with ours as he also seeks the downfall of Stevens."

"Sounds promising, what's next?" Reyes inquired.

"Second, we have Zaria Nix. She's a human, but not your ordinary one. A brilliant scientist, she has been on the run ever since she refused to work on a bioweapon project for Stevens," Syv continued.

Reyes nodded, "Two down, who's the third?"

"Third is Quil Tavash. A Zelarian. They are skilled in manipulating energies and Quil is a former space pirate. However, he turned against his crew when he realized that they were involved in smuggling artifacts for Stevens."

"And the fourth?" asked Reyes.

"Lastly, a Sylphian named Lyra Windrider. Sylphians are known for their aerial combat skills, and she has a personal vendetta against Stevens for destroying her homeland," finished Syv.

Reyes turned to Moore, who was standing nearby, "We need these people. Prep the ship. We're going on a recruitment drive."

Moore smiled, "Yes, Commander"

"Commander" Syv questionably said.

"Yes, what is it" Reyes said as he raised a brow

"There's one more I failed to mention, a unique entity known as One. It's a highly advanced AI that gained self-awareness and now operates independently in the outer rim. It may not sympathize with our cause, but it's unlikely to support Stevens either, given his manipulation of AI for his own ends."

"Yes, interesting, I'll keep a note of it" Reyes said with his arms firmly crossed.

"Alright Syv" Reyes said. "we have some folks lines up, set course for the Drakkan homeworld, Rak'thor Kresh being a warlord could mean he had dealings with Stevens, anyone with info on him is worth the trip."

"Affirmative, Commander," Syv responded with robotic efficiency. The Bushido's engines hummed as the ship smoothly changed course and accelerated toward Chiron IV.

◆ ◆ ◆

In the briefing room, Reyes stood at the head of the table, his hands folded in front of him. His crew - Moore, McKinley, Dr. M'doius, and Vela - were all gathered around, waiting for him to begin the briefing.

"We're setting a course for Chrion IV," he began. "Our objective there is Rak'thor Kresh, a formidable Drakkan warrior. He was once a warlord, but was dethroned, and now he's out for revenge."

Moore leaned forward, her eyebrows furrowed. "Revenge against whom?"

"Stevens," Reyes replied, his voice heavy. "Stevens helped orchestrate Kresh's downfall, and now they want vengeance."

McKinley chuckled from his seat. "So we've got a common enemy then. Sounds like this Kresh could be a valuable ally."

Dr. M'doius nodded her agreement. "Indeed, his strength and combat skills could prove crucial in our mission. Plus, his personal vendetta against Stevens could further motivate him."

Vela, who had been silent until now, finally spoke up. "And if this Kresh refuses to join us? What then?"

Reyes gave her a hard look. "Then we make him see the bigger picture. We make him understand that this isn't just about personal revenge. It's about the survival of the galaxy. Kresh can be a part of that, or he can stand in our way."

With the plan in place, the crew dispersed, each returning to their duties with renewed determination. The mission was clear - enlist Kresh's help in their fight against Stevens, one way or another.

◆ ◆ ◆

The Bushido approached Chiron IV, Reyes and his team prepared to disembark. They were fully armed and ready for any eventuality, as the Drakkan were known for their martial prowess and not to be taken lightly.

Chiron IV was a rugged, mountainous world, with thick forests and flowing rivers. The Bushido landed in a clearing near a small Drakkan settlement. Reyes and his team descended the ship's ramp and were immediately met by a group of heavily armed Drakkans.

One of them, a towering figure with four muscular scaly arms and wearing intricate battle armor, stepped forward. His fierce eyes studied Reyes and his crew.

"I am Rak'thor Kresh," he announced in a deep, rumbling voice. "What brings off-worlders to our planet? phft, and humans at that!" he scoffed

Reyes stood firm, meeting his gaze. "I am Commander Eli Reyes of the United Federation of Sol. We've come to seek your help. We heard you might have a slight problem here on Chiron Reyes let the veiled challenge hang in the air for a moment, the tension as palpable as the electric charge in the mountain air. "We heard a rumor that the one who took your throne is causing trouble in the cosmos, trouble we want to stop. But we're going to need your help to do it."

Rak'thor Kresh's reptilian eyes narrowed, his lips drawing back over a row of razor-sharp teeth in a feral grin. "Ah, the betrayer, Stevens. I've been waiting for someone like you, Reyes. But why should we trust you? Why should we believe you can succeed where we failed?"

A silence fell over the landing area, punctuated only by the distant cry of Chiron IV's indigenous creatures. The Drakkan warriors and Reyes's team both waited for his response, all aware of the significance of this moment. It was not just a question of trust, but of pride and alliances, of ancient enmities and uneasy partnerships.

"We're your best chance to reclaim what was taken from you," Reyes said, holding the Drakkan's gaze, "and we have enemies in common. Stevens, the usurper, has wreaked havoc on more than just your world. He is a threat to all of us. My team and I are determined to stop him."

Reyes gestured to his companions, each standing tall, their own determination clear on their faces. "This is Moore, Mckinley, Dr. M'doius, and Vela. We've fought together, bled together, and we stand united against Stevens. Help us, and we promise to do all we can to restore your rightful place."

Kresh looked at each of them, his predatory gaze assessing their mettle. After a long moment, he turned his attention back to Reyes. "Very well, human. We will listen. But be warned, we Drakkans do not give our trust lightly, and we expect no less than honor in our alliances. Betray us, and you will face the full might of the Drakkan race."

As they followed Rak'thor Kresh deeper into the Drakkan settlement, each member of Reyes' team was well aware that they were venturing into unknown territory, the weight of their mission, and the delicate balance of this new alliance heavy on their shoulders. The meeting with the Drakkan could very well dictate the fate of the entire galaxy. The torch-lit interior of the Drakkan settlement reflected the stark resilience of its people, its rugged architecture carved from the mountainside. At the heart of this society was a vast, cavernous hall, encircled by tiered seating filled with muscular Drakkan warriors. At one end, upon an imposing throne, sat the usurper.

Kresh stood at the entrance of the hall, his gaze locked with Nar'shal's. His voice boomed through the silent expanse. "Nar'shal," he called out, "I, Rak'thor Kresh, challenge you. You've tarnished our honor by allying with the off-worlder, Stevens."

Nar'shal, from his lofty seat, glared down at Kresh. "You dare challenge me, Rak'thor?" he retorted, his voice echoing in the cavern. "You, who lost his throne and was exiled?"

The crowd of Drakkan murmured, their attention riveted on the unfolding drama. Reyes and his team held their silence, aware of their status as outsiders in this critical, cultural event. Their role here was not to intervene, but to observe and support their ally, Kresh.

"Yes, Nar'shal," Kresh answered firmly, "I challenge you. Not just for my own honor, but for the integrity of all Drakkan, which you've besmirched under Stevens' influence."

Nar'shal leaned back on his throne, his eyes gleaming with contempt. "Very well, Kresh," he announced, "We'll settle this at dawn."

The chamber reverberated with the approval of the assembled Drakkan. The upcoming dawn would bear witness to a defining moment in Drakkan society and for Reyes and his team, a pivotal point in their mission to defeat Stevens.

As the echoes of the assembly dissipated, Kresh turned to Reyes and his team, his fierce eyes softening. "You have shown bravery in standing by me," he acknowledged. "You shall rest here tonight, among my kin and me."

As Kresh led them through winding stone corridors, they arrived at a large chamber, warm and welcoming, lit by the soft glow of burning torches. A sizable group of Drakkans, loyalists to Kresh, had gathered. Laughter and the clinking of cups filled the air.

Kresh welcomed them into a spacious chamber, "Might not be the Bushido, but it'll do for the night," Kresh joked, showcasing a rare glimpse of levity. The room was filled with warmth and the promise of camaraderie, Reyes and his team found themselves enveloped by a merry crowd of Drakkans. Despite their foreignness, the barriers between them seemed to melt away in the hearty ambiance. Kresh, the muscles of his face pulling into an uncharacteristic grin, raised his glass high. "Commander, how about a friendly bout of our local sport?" His eyes gleamed with mischievousness. "A Torga nectar drinking competition. Do you accept the challenge?"

Reyes, meeting the warlord's gaze, replied with a nod and a growing smirk. "Well alright Kresh, challenge accepted. I hope this nectar is as potent as your legends say."

"We shall surely see!" Kresh said, as Laughter erupted, cups clinked, and the competition was underway. As each round passed, more participants swayed, stumbled, and ultimately surrendered to the strong, heady effects of the nectar. In the end, it was just Reyes and Kresh, both teetering on the edge of coherence. But as the final round was poured, it was Kresh whose hand faltered, his glass tipping and nectar spilling. The hall burst into a wave of laughter and applause as Kresh conceded defeat.

Kresh, his speech slurring, struggled to form the words, "I... I didn't see this coming," he managed to say, a round of laughter enveloping him. With a shaky hand, he raised his glass to Reyes. "Commander... you... you won... won my respect," he slurred, his words barely discernible. The word 'friend' was attempted, but it drowned in another bout of laughter. As for Reyes, words were beyond him at this point. Instead, his response was a wide, cheeky grin. A victor's grin that was wild, uninhibited, and infectious. Despite his inebriation, his eyes sparkled with triumphant mischief, eliciting another wave of hearty laughter from the onlookers. The night wore on, the room filled with merry chatter, and the off-worlders found a sense of unity with their Drakkan hosts. The night ended on a high note, the tensions of the upcoming dawn momentarily forgotten. The party went late into the night, their laughter and merriment echoing in the stone hallways. They knew that the coming day would bring its challenges, but for now, they reveled in their newfound camaraderie.

◆ ◆ ◆

As dawn's first light pierced through the cracks of the room, the aftermath of the night's festivities came into view. The once lively room was now a mosaic of scattered Drakkans and humans, slumped over tables, propped against walls, or stretched out on the floor.

Kresh, the formidable warlord, was snoring loudly. He had claimed a large, ornate bed for himself but was sprawled across it sideways, a peaceful expression on his face in contrast to his usual stern demeanor. His loyal followers were strewn about, their powerful forms collapsed in various states of sleep and unconsciousness. Slowly stirring, Reyes managed to sit up from his spot on a bench, shaking his head to clear the remaining fog of the Torga nectar. His wild grin had mellowed to a satisfied smirk. With the morning's clarity, he took a moment to appreciate the rare tranquility of the scene. Then, shaking off the last remnants of drowsiness, he stood and began waking his crew. Moore was curled up on a nearby couch, a small smile gracing her face even as she woke. Vela had somehow perched herself high up on a rafter, her bird-like traits evident even in sleep. She woke with a start, flapping down to join the others. Mckinley, after being shaken awake, groaned dramatically but managed to stand with a little assistance. Once his crew was collected, Reyes turned his attention to the sleeping warlord. Approaching the bed, he nudged Kresh, "Wake up, big guy. We've got a duel to prepare for."

With a groan and a mighty stretch, Kresh opened his eyes. For a moment, he looked confused, but then the memory of the impending duel seemed to hit him. Sitting up, he met Reyes' gaze and nodded, "Right, we've got a score to settle."

With their leader awake, the remaining Drakkans began to stir, rising and readying themselves for the challenges of the day. Despite the previous night's indulgence, a palpable air of determination filled the room. They all knew the importance of the duel at dawn and were ready to face it head-on.

CHAPTER 15

Reyes extended a hand to Kresh, pulling him up from the bed. The room was beginning to fill with activity as everyone scrambled to prepare.
"Alright, everyone, let's get to it," Reyes commanded, his voice echoing through the chamber.
Moore shook her head clear of the lingering Torga nectar effects and asked, "What's the plan, Commander?"
"We have to ensure Kresh is at his best. The duel is a matter of hours away," Reyes answered, glancing towards Kresh who was now on his feet, stretching out his muscles.
Vela, her eyes now sharp and focused, piped up, "We should scout the area where the duel is taking place. It would be good to have some knowledge of the terrain."
"Good thinking, Vela," Reyes agreed, giving her a nod of approval.
Dr. M'doius, who'd been oddly silent till now, added, "We should also ensure Kresh is in optimal health. I can run a quick check-up, make sure the nectar has left his system completely."
"Excellent, doctor. Meanwhile, Mckinley, you're with me. We'll go over the rules of the duel with the local officials, ensure there are no surprises," Reyes instructed, turning towards Mckinley who gave a quick salute in acknowledgement.
Kresh, his voice gruff from sleep and drink, said, "I appreciate

your help, friends. I did not think I would ever duel again, but if I must, I am glad to have you at my side."

With their tasks clear, the team dispersed. The hum of activity filled the room as everyone prepared for the high stakes of the upcoming duel. As the day wore on, the dawn's tranquility gave way to the tense anticipation of the fight that was to come.

◆ ◆ ◆

The sun was high in the sky when the distinct sound of the Drakkan horns reverberated through the settlement, a deep, resonant tone that echoed off the mountainsides. It was time. The duel was about to begin.

The crew, along with Kresh, who now looked every bit the formidable warlord in his gleaming battle armor, left the chamber, their boots echoing on the stone floors. The doors opened to a spectacle outside - the entire settlement had gathered to witness the duel.

As they made their way to the arena, Kresh turned to Reyes and his team. His voice was firm, filled with grim resolve. "No matter what happens, you've done more for me than I could've asked. For that, I am grateful."

Reyes nodded at him, his face stern, "You're not going into this alone, Kresh. We're with you."

As they entered the battlefield, Nar'Shal was already there, waiting. His armor was darker, his expression scornful. His four eyes scanned the crowd before settling on Kresh. A cruel smile formed on his face as he readied his weapon.

There was an electric tension in the air as the crowd fell silent. The only sounds were the distant rustle of the wind through the trees and the occasional screech of some alien bird. It was a world holding its breath, waiting for the clash that was to come. Kresh and Nar'Shal locked eyes, the unspoken challenge hanging between them. This was more than a duel for leadership; it was a fight for honor, for vengeance, and for the future of their people. The horn sounded once more, echoing the start of the duel. Two titans faced each other, each prepared to fight until only one remained standing. The moment the second horn's echo faded, Nar'Shal lunged at Kresh, his dual-bladed weapon cutting through the air with a vicious swiftness. Kresh met his assault head-on, parrying the strike with his own weapon, a massive hammer-like instrument that shook the ground with its impact. Their battle was a symphony of clanging metal, roars, and grunts. Each attack and counterattack was met with resounding cheers and gasps from the onlooking crowd. Reyes and his crew watched in silent anticipation, their eyes never leaving the dueling pair.

Kresh, utilizing his strength, managed to land a powerful blow that sent Nar'Shal sprawling. The crowd erupted in cheers. However, the victory was short-lived. Nar'Shal, undeterred, sprang back to his feet, a savage determination painted across his features. Blood dripped down from a wound on his forehead, staining his armor, but he seemed to barely notice it.

The duel escalated, becoming a dance of death, each combatant giving their all. Nar'Shal, faster and more agile, darted around Kresh, his blades leaving a trail of gory scratches on Kresh's armor. But Kresh, undeterred, kept pushing forward, his brute strength meeting Nar'Shal's speed head-on.

At one point, Kresh managed to close the distance between them, locking Nar'Shal in a vice grip. Nar'Shal writhed, using one of his blades to cut across Kresh's forearm, the other stabbing into Kresh's side. A roar of pain echoed from Kresh, yet he didn't let go. Instead, he swung his hammer, landing a devastating blow to Nar'Shal's side.

Both warriors, now bleeding heavily, fought with a desperation and ferocity that had the crowd on edge. It was a gruesome sight, yet none could look away. The field was now a macabre painting of blood and alien sand, bearing witness to a battle for honor, fought with everything they had. Under the merciless sun, the clash of the titans raged on. It was a scene of raw, primal energy, a testament to the indomitable spirit of the Drakkan species. It was a spectacle none present would forget. As the duel wore on, both warriors began to show signs of fatigue. Blood was now soaking their respective armors, each breath was a labored gasp, yet neither of them would yield. Their determination was mirrored in their fierce glares as they circled each other, taking a momentary reprieve before launching into the next round.

In the crowd, silence reigned. Everyone was holding their breath, their eyes glued to the spectacle before them. The very air seemed to thicken with anticipation as Kresh and Nar'Shal locked eyes, a silent understanding passing between them. It was time for the final blow.

Much like a scene from an old samurai standoff, they stood still, the tension between them palpable. Time seemed to slow as they stared each other down, the entire world shrinking down to just the two of them.

And then, in a blink-and-you'll-miss-it moment, Kresh moved. His weapon, which he'd been holding in a defensive position, swung with a speed and precision that belied his size. It was a swift, clean strike, one that Nar'Shal didn't see coming until it was too late.

With a final, sickening thud, Nar'Shal's head was cleanly severed from his body, flying through the air before landing a few feet away. His lifeless body crumbled to the ground, his reign over the Drakkans ending in a pool of his own blood.

The arena was eerily quiet for a few heart-stopping seconds, everyone frozen in shock at the sudden and dramatic conclusion. And then, the silence was shattered by an eruption of cheers. The crowd roared their approval, their relief, their triumphant joy. Kresh, their rightful leader, had won. The deposed warlord had reclaimed his throne, not by conspiracy or treachery, but by the sheer force of his will and might.

Reyes and his team let out a breath they didn't realize they had been holding. Their eyes were wide, their hearts pounded in their chests as they absorbed the shocking climax of the duel. They had seen Kresh at his most formidable, at his most savage, and it was a sight they would never forget.

Kresh, victorious but battered, moved with a grim determination. His wounds ached, his muscles screamed in protest, but he held his head high, his pride and honor untarnished. His journey to the throne was as challenging as the duel itself, each step seeming like a battle won. The crowd parted to form a path, their cheers echoing his victory, their respect palpable in their awestruck silence.

Reaching the throne, a mighty construct of stone and bone, Kresh turned to face his people. His eyes scanned the sea of faces before him, all eyes fixed on their newly reinstated leader. His gaze was stern but filled with a softness, an understanding, that only a leader who had walked amongst his people could possess. Drawing a labored breath, Kresh raised his arm, signaling for silence. Gradually, the cheers died down, replaced by an anticipatory hush. When he spoke, his voice was deep and resonant, echoing across the gathered throng.

"Drakkan, brothers and sisters, we stand today at a crossroads," he began, his voice filled with the weight of his words. "We have seen treachery, we have seen betrayal, but today we have also seen justice."

He paused, letting his words sink in, then continued. "I did not fight this duel for personal gain. I did not shed blood for glory or fame. I did it for us, for our people. For the future of our clan. Nar'Shal's rule was one of oppression and deception. He betrayed us all, but today we reclaim our honor."

Kresh's gaze swept across his audience. "We are Drakkan! We are strong, we are resilient. But we are not just warriors, we are also people of honor, of integrity. We must never forget that. Under my leadership, we will forge a path of unity, strength, and prosperity. Together, we will rebuild." His eyes glinted with determination. "I am not your ruler, I am your brother. Your voice, your strength, is as crucial as mine. Together, we are stronger, and together, we shall stand against all adversities." The crowd erupted into deafening cheers and applause, their roars echoing through the mountains. The sun shone brightly on Chiron IV, casting long shadows and illuminating the scene before them - a leader, battered but unbowed, standing tall amidst his people. Victorious, Kresh stood tall and raised his weapon high above his head. His eyes met Reyes', and in that moment, there was a sense of understanding, a mutual respect forged in the fires of battle. The sun glinted off his armor, off the blood splattered across his body, painting a heroic picture of a leader reborn. He let the cheers wash over him, his chest swelling with pride. After a moment, he raised his hand once more, asking for silence. The noise slowly died down, leaving a serene stillness.

"I stand here before you," he continued, "Not just as your leader, but also as someone humbled and indebted. Today's victory is not just mine. It was made possible by the courage and determination of others, of outsiders who chose to help us despite our differences."

He turned then to look at Reyes and his team. "Eli Reyes, Sarah Moore, Harry McKinley, Dr. Aeesse M'doius, and Vela Sulmus... I am proud to call them friends." His eyes connected with each of theirs, an acknowledgement, a silent thank you.

"Look at them, Drakkan!" He gestured towards the team with a sweep of his arm. "They came from far beyond our stars, from different races, different cultures, yet they stood by us, helped us reclaim our honor. They are a testament to the unity we can achieve, the bridges we can build."

He let his arm drop, once more looking out at the crowd. "Let this day be a reminder to all of us, that strength is not just in might, but also in unity. In friendship, in understanding. Our friends have shown us that. I am proud to stand with them, as much as I am proud to stand with you."

"And so, I ask you to extend your respect to them as well. They are our allies, our friends. They have earned their place among us, and I am certain that together, we will face whatever comes our way."

Once more, the air was filled with the deafening sound of cheers. Reyes and his team stood there, the weight of Kresh's words sinking in. They looked at the sea of Drakkan faces, the respect and gratitude mirrored in their eyes, and knew that they had made a difference, had created an ally in a place once ruled by a foe.

For the first time in what felt like forever, they were hopeful. They had made a stand, fought a battle, and emerged victorious. It was a small step, but it was a step nonetheless, and it gave them the hope they needed to continue their mission. Under the bright sun of Chiron IV, with the cheers of the Drakkan echoing in their ears, Reyes and his team looked at each other, a shared understanding passing between them. They had a long way to go, but they were ready, ready to face whatever the universe had in store for them. Together. Kresh's speech drew to a close and the celebratory cheers filled the air, he walked over to Reyes and his crew. His strides were strong and purposeful despite his injuries.

"Commander Reyes," Kresh began, a trace of amusement glimmering in his eyes, "Enjoy the festivities today. There's plenty of Torga nectar flowing. But remember, it's not a competition this time," he added with a hearty laugh.

Reyes, still feeling the effects of the previous night's drinking competition, responded with a grin, "I think I've had my fair share of Torga nectar for one lifetime, Kresh."

The entire group chuckled at their exchange, the camaraderie and mutual respect palpable among them.

Kresh's gaze then shifted towards the sky, a thoughtful expression on his face. "Tomorrow, I will join you aboard the Bushido," he declared. "There's a fight ahead, and I am ready to stand with you."

"We welcome your aid, Kresh," Moore chimed in, her voice firm and sincere. "Your victory today was inspiring."

"And don't worry about the Torga nectar on board," joked Mckinley, his eyes twinkling mischievously. "We'll make sure to stock up on some water."

Their laughter echoed amidst the festivities, a promise of unity and friendship that would persist through the trials ahead. For now, they would revel in their victory, the joy and triumph of the day washing over them. But when dawn broke, they would set their sights on their mission once again, their resolve stronger than ever.

CHAPTER 16

The Bushido hummed with life as it traversed the star-lit expanse. In the crew hall, a room that was now unmistakably Drakkan in nature had been taken over by Kresh. The room was filled with various items he'd brought with him from Chiron IV - intricately carved statuettes of fierce Drakkan warriors, woven tapestries depicting epic battles, and even a few Drakkan weapons displayed with pride.

As Reyes stepped into the room, the scent of a strange incense filled his nostrils. The room was dimly lit, creating a soothing ambiance. Kresh was seated on a low stool, deeply engrossed in polishing one of his weapons.

"Kresh," Reyes began, leaning against the doorframe, "I see you're settling in well."

Kresh looked up from his work, the corners of his mouth lifting in a small smile. "I am indeed, Commander," he responded, placing the weapon down on the table in front of him. "These reminders of home bring comfort during these unfamiliar travels."

Reyes nodded, appreciating Kresh's sentiment. "It's important to carry a piece of home with us," he agreed, "Especially when we're so far away."

Kresh nodded, his gaze turning back to his artifacts. "I am ready for what lies ahead, Reyes. My strength and loyalty are with you and this crew."

"And we are grateful for it, Kresh," Reyes assured him, clasping his shoulder in a comradely manner. "We're all in this together."

"I'll leave you to it then, Kresh." Reyes said as he left Kresh to his solitude, feeling a sense of resolve filled the air. The team was slowly coming together, their shared mission forging bonds of trust and respect.

◆ ◆ ◆

Ascending to the bridge, the subtle hum of the Bushido's engines provided a familiar, comforting backdrop. The room was awash with the glow of various displays, casting a soft light on the crew manning their stations.

In the midst of it all stood Moore, her gaze focused on the holographic star chart projected in front of her. She glanced up as Reyes entered, a hint of a smile crossing her lips. "Commander," she greeted, straightening up.

"Moore," Reyes nodded back, approaching her side. There was a pause as they both admired the countless stars and galaxies projected in front of them. It was a sight that never failed to amaze.

"You did well on Chiron IV," he told her, breaking the silence. "Your diplomacy played a key role in winning over Kresh."

Moore shrugged modestly, "I did what was needed. We're a team, after all."

Reyes glanced at her, the soft lighting illuminating her features. There was a strength in her eyes, a resolve that matched his own. "We are," he agreed, his voice a bit softer. "And a good one, at that."

The moment hung in the air, the unsaid words lingering between them. It was interrupted by the sound of Syv's mechanical voice over the comms.

"Commander, your orders?" the Tranakaran pilot inquired.

Reyes turned away from Moore, clearing his throat. "Set a course for Europa, Syv," he commanded. "We've got another recruit to pick up. This Zaria Nix could perhaps, give us some insight about this bio-weapon Stevens plans to develop."

As the Bushido shifted its course, Reyes felt the anticipation build. With each new ally they gained, they were one step closer to taking down Stevens. But for now, he had to focus on the mission at hand: finding Zaria Nix.

"Commander, Europa isn't the same as when I left it," Moore began, her voice holding a note of caution. "The planet has changed... and not for the better."

Reyes turned back towards her, curiosity piqued. "What do you mean?"

She sighed, her gaze focused on the star chart. "It's run by thugs now. The largest settlement, Zulu, has a massive club where their leader resides. There not the type to appreciate Federation officers."

He nodded, taking in her words. There was a seriousness in her tone he wasn't used to.

"We'll need to tread lightly, then," he decided, glancing back at the chart.

"You always do," Moore remarked, a hint of sarcasm coloring her words.

Reyes grinned at her, "Is that concern I hear in your voice, Moore?"

She rolled her eyes at his joke, but her lips curved into a smile, "Just making sure you're prepared, Commander."

Reyes laughed lightly, "Noted. We'll handle it, Moore. We always do."

"As much as I'd love to keep analyzing star charts, I'm calling it a night," Reyes announced, fatigue finally catching up to him.

Syv's mechanical voice came over the comm again, "Rest well, Commander."

Reyes turned to Moore, seeing a hint of hesitation in her eyes. "You good here, Moore?" he asked.
She paused for a moment, meeting his gaze. "Actually, would you mind if I walked with you?"
He raised a brow in surprise, then chuckled. "Isn't that against Federation guidelines?" he joked, referring to the traditional military rules around fraternization.
Moore shrugged, a playful glint in her eyes, "Who's going to report us?"
Reyes laughed, shaking his head. "Fair point. Alright, let's go."
With that, they left the bridge together, their banter fading as the doors slid shut behind them. The ship continued humming gently as it made its way through the endless cosmos towards Europa. The journey was far from over, but for the moment, they were content.
As the two walked down the corridor, Moore broke the silence. "Do you ever think about it, Reyes? That we might be living in our last days?"
Reyes looked at her, surprised by the sudden heaviness of the conversation. He shrugged. "I suppose it crosses my mind, but it doesn't do any good to dwell on it."
In his quarters, they settled in comfortably. Reyes brought out a couple of drinks from his personal collection, offering one to Moore.
"Here's to... not dwelling on the end of the world," he raised his glass in a toast.
She chuckled, clinking her glass against his. "I'll drink to that."
As they sipped their drinks, Reyes leaned back in his chair, his gaze drifting around his quarters. "You know, I never thought I'd end up here," he said quietly, "A soldier, sure. But leading a mission like this? It's... a lot."
Moore nodded, her own gaze focused on the golden liquid in her glass. "I understand. I grew up dreaming of exploring the stars,

not running from a maniac trying to end them all."

Reyes chuckled lightly, "From exploring the cosmos to saving it. Quite the career shift, huh?"

Their laughter faded into a comfortable silence. It was Moore who broke it again, her voice barely above a whisper, "Do you ever wonder what we'd be doing, if things were different?"

"All the time," Reyes admitted. He took a deep breath, pausing as he gathered his thoughts. "I think, in another life, I'd be a simple freighter pilot. Just me and the open stars, no wars, no federation, no end of the world looming over our heads."

Moore looked at him then, a soft smile playing on her lips. "That sounds nice. I'd probably be an astronomer. Nothing fancy, just me, a telescope, and the endless mysteries of the universe."

Finally, Reyes looked into Moore's eyes, his voice softening, "Sarah, I...," he hesitated, his gaze dropping to her lips. Moore, reading his intentions, closed the small gap between them, capturing his lips with her own. It was a gentle kiss, a soft exploration that spoke volumes more than words ever could. Their initial hesitation melted away, replaced by a growing passion. The intensity of their kiss increased, hands tentatively reaching out, tracing lines and curves. Their breaths mingled, hearts pounded, and bodies yearned for closeness. With a shared understanding, they made their way to the bed, their movements synchronized, there was a palpable excitement and tenderness between them. Moore's fingers traced the contours of Reyes' face, as if memorizing every detail, while his hands found their way to the small of her back, pulling her closer. In the dim light, Moore's skin seemed to glow, and Reyes felt a thrill at the sensation of her body against his. The closeness was electrifying, each touch a spark that set them both aflame. Reyes whispered into Moore's ear, his voice heavy with emotion, "I never thought I'd find someone who could understand the weight of the stars on my shoulders." Moore looked into his eyes and smiled, her breath warm against his cheek. "And I never imagined finding someone brave enough to share that burden," she whispered back. As they fell onto the bed, the soft fabric embracing them, they moved with a kind of urgency, as if trying to make up for the time they had not acknowledged their feelings for each other. They explored each other with their hands, their lips, their very breaths, and for a time, there was nothing but them and the rhythm of their hearts beating together. They surrendered themselves fully, making promises without words, and finding a comfort that only kindred spirits could share. The starlight bathing them in its gentle embrace seemed to whisper secrets of the universe, and in that moment, they felt as if they could take on anything. Wrapped in each other's arms, they eventually fell into a deep and contented sleep, their souls entwined as they journeyed through the night. In the cocoon of the commander's quarters, with the vastness of space as their witness, Reyes and Moore had found solace and connection. For a fleeting moment, they had created a sanctuary amidst the turmoil of their mission, a memory they would carry like a precious treasure.

◆ ◆ ◆

A gentle chime broke through the tranquil silence of the commander's quarters, pulling Reyes from his deep sleep. His hand fumbled for the communicator lying on the nightstand, his eyes still heavy with sleep. On the screen, Syv's face materialized.
"Commander, we are approaching Europa," the Tranakaran pilot reported, his speech patterns rhythmic and mechanical.
"Alright, Syv. Take us in, to Zulu," Reyes responded, rubbing the sleep from his eyes. "We'll start there."
"Understood, Commander."
Reyes ended the communication, laying the device back onto the

nightstand. He turned to look at Moore, who was still lost in peaceful slumber. A lock of her hair fell across her face, her breaths deep and even. In the soft morning light that filtered through the windows, she looked serene.

For a moment, Reyes simply watched her sleep, his heart filled with a warmth he hadn't known in a long time. He carefully moved the lock of hair from her face, then, gently planting a kiss on her forehead, he quietly rose from the bed, not wanting to disturb her.

Dressed and ready, he cast one last lingering look at Moore before stepping out of the quarters, his heart swelling with a mixture of affection and concern. The day ahead promised challenges, and he only hoped that the warmth of the previous night would provide the strength they both needed to face them.

The commander made his way to the bridge, the hum of the engines changing pitch as they neared Europa, it was alive with activity. The buzz of the ship's systems, the hushed tones of conversation, and the occasional burst of laughter filled the air. Nestled in a corner, Mckinley and Kresh shared a hearty conversation, their booming voices occasionally rising above the general din.

As Reyes entered, Mckinley, upon noticing him, straightened immediately, his burly figure easily dwarfing the commander. A well of mirth still lingered in his eyes as he saluted Reyes. "Commander," he greeted, a trace of his Liverpudlian accent slipping through.

"At ease, Mckinley," Reyes replied, a soft smile curving at the corners of his mouth. The sight of his crew sharing a laugh eased a portion of the burden off his shoulders.

Mckinley lowered his salute and glanced around the bridge, his brow furrowed in thought. "Say, haven't seen Officer Moore around. Usually, she's the first one here," he observed, his eyes finally landing on Reyes with a quizzical expression.

Before Reyes could answer, a light seemed to click in Mckinley's eyes, and his broad face split into a knowing grin. "Ah," he said, his voice layered with amusement. "I see how it is. Commander and the First Officer, eh? Staying up late, reviewing... Federation guidelines, were we?"

Despite the flush creeping up his neck, Reyes managed a dry chuckle, his lips twitching into a smirk. "That's enough, Mckinley. Can it," he said, though the twinkle in his eyes betrayed his amusement. The air in the bridge felt a little lighter as Reyes joined his crew, the shared laughter a small respite before they plunged back into their mission. Reyes turned his attention to the holographic display of Europa, glancing between it and his crew. "Since you two seem to be up and about, you'll be joining me in Zulu," he announced, his gaze flicking between Mckinley and Kresh. "Word is that they're not too keen on 'Fedies' down there." He used the colloquial term for Federation personnel with a hint of a smirk.

Mckinley's grin widened, while Kresh simply gave a solemn nod, his scaly brow quirking in interest.

"I'm going to need two 'bodyguards'," Reyes continued, a hint of dry humor in his tone. "So, prepare yourselves. We'll be landing soon."

"Sounds like fun, Commander," Mckinley responded with an enthusiastic clap of his hands, "We'll be the best bodyguards you've ever had. Right, Kresh?"

The Drakkan let out a low, rumbling chuckle, his multiple arms flexing instinctively. "We will ensure your safety, Commander," he assured, his tone surprisingly gentle for a warrior of his stature.

"Good," Reyes nodded, feeling a renewed sense of determination. "We've got a scientist to find, and a mission to complete. Let's get to it."

With that, the three of them prepared for their expedition on

Europa, unaware of the events that were soon to unfold.

CHAPTER 17

Just as the trio was preparing, the door slid open, and in walked Moore and Vela. There was a split-second pause as Moore and Reyes exchanged a glance, a hint of last night's intimacy lingering. McKinley, ever perceptive, spotted it and raised his eyebrows at Reyes, a playful grin spreading on his face.
"Alright, McKinley," Reyes said, his tone light despite the warning in his eyes, "Eyes on the mission."
McKinley only laughed, turning his attention to Moore. "Aye, Commander. No harm meant."
Moore cleared her throat, a faint blush on her cheeks before her professional demeanor took over. "Zulu is controlled by the Trask gang," she began, pacing as she spoke. "They run everything, from the smallest shops to the largest clubs. The leader, Garrick Trask, resides in the club named The Black Hole. It's likely that's where we'll find Zaria."
Vela chimed in, her hands folded in front of her. "You three will have communicators on you. Should anything go awry, you just need to press the panic button. We'll be monitoring your vitals from the ship. The moment we see any anomaly, we'll pull you out."
There was a moment of silence as everyone took in the information. "It won't come to that," Reyes said finally. "We know what we're walking into, and we're prepared. Let's get this

show on the road."

◆ ◆ ◆

Making their way through the bustling landing terminal of Zulu, the trio caught the attention of two burly guards who moved to intercept them. Their arms were crossed over their chests, and they bore the tattoo of a black hole – the symbol of the Trask gang.
"Hold up there, Commander Reyes," the taller one said, a sneer playing on his lips. His gaze flicked over to Kresh and McKinley, then back to Reyes.
Reyes arched an eyebrow at the recognition. "So, you know who I am then?"
"Of course, we had you tagged the moment you entered Europa orbit," the guard responded, a sense of self-satisfaction seeping into his tone. "You're not as subtle as you like to think, Commander."
The other guard stepped forward, his gaze hard. "Trask wants to know what brings a Federation commander to Europa. I strongly suggest you go to The Black Hole and present yourself."
Reyes held up a hand. "Ease up on the attitude," he said, his tone firm. "I'm not here to cause any problems."
The guard scoffed, crossing his arms over his chest. "Yeah, well, ships seem to explode around you, Commander. Explosions tend to cause problems, The Black Hole... now." Both guards turned and walked away from the trio. They were met with the mischievous grin of McKinley. "Puffed-up popinjays, those two. Muscles packed with more gas than grit, I'd wager."
Reyes couldn't hold back a soft chuckle, shaking his head in amusement. "That's enough, McKinley. We don't need any unnecessary confrontation here."
McKinley gave a good-natured shrug, his grin unwavering. Kresh, on the other hand, had been silent, his four eyes sharp

and alert, taking in their new environment with an unreadable expression.

The trio navigated their way through the bustling streets of Zulu, their destination looming ahead – the Black Hole. This imposing structure was a cacophony of vibrant lights and pulsating rhythms that threatened to drown out the city's own life beat.

As they neared, the extensive queue of hopeful patrons caught their attention. The line twisted and turned like a coiled serpent, its length disappearing into the maze of the city behind them.

A bouncer, mountainous in his stature and as immovable as the building behind him, stood in their path. Reyes, adopting an air of confident authority, addressed the colossal gatekeeper. "We've got an appointment with Trask," he announced. "He should be expecting us."

A long pause followed as the bouncer studied them, his eyes lingering on each of their faces. McKinley, under the bouncer's scrutiny, tried to ease the tension. "Lovely night for a friendly visit, isn't it?"

However, the bouncer remained stoic, not bothering to respond to McKinley's jest. After what felt like an eternity, he finally spoke. "Trask will see you. Right this way."

◆ ◆ ◆

The club was a kaleidoscope of neon lights and riotous sounds, a melting pot of sights and experiences that bombarded the senses. Above, dancers suspended in cages spun and twirled, captivating the entranced patrons below. Multiple dance floors, each with its own unique ambience, pulsed with the rhythm of the bass-heavy music, the energy of the crowd as palpable as the air they breathed. The bar, a majestic hub in the center, boasted an array of exotic drinks that glowed in all colors under the fluorescent lights.

Against this backdrop of vibrant chaos, the bouncer led the trio, navigating through the labyrinth of sound and light, towards a more private area. A staircase emerged from the crowd, leading them up into an elevated VIP section that commanded an expansive view of the club below.

Seated at the pinnacle was Trask, a figure of authority amidst the revelry. Flanked by two guards, he watched the club below with an air of detached interest.

As they neared, one of the guards raised a hand, halting McKinley and Kresh. The second guard advanced on Reyes, a scanner in hand. A quick sweep confirmed what they already knew – Reyes was unarmed.

"He's clean," the guard announced, stepping back to resume his position beside Trask.

At the affirmation, Trask gestured for Reyes to approach. His eyes, calculating and shrewd, assessed the Federation Commander with intrigue. "Commander Reyes," he began, his voice slicing through the cacophony, "What brings a Federation lap dog into my club?" Reyes met Trask's gaze unflinchingly, the ambient noise of the club fading into a blur as he focused on the task at hand. He detailed their mission, expressing his interest in locating Zaria Nix for her potential help in the fight against Stevens.

Trask listened, his face impassive. When Reyes finished, Trask leaned back in his chair, considering the Commander before him. "Zaria Nix...yes, she is here on Europa," he confirmed, a note of caution entering his voice. "However, she's currently working on a cure for the outbreak in District Six. The area is quarantined. It's a wasteland down there, Commander. No man's land."

Reyes took the news in stride, a resolute determination settling on his features. He had faced worse odds in his time with the Federation. "I appreciate the concern, Trask," he said, a hint of a smile touching his lips. "But I've been in my fair share of no man's land before. We'll handle it."

Trask regarded him for a moment longer, then nodded, signaling the end of the conversation. "Very well, Commander. Just don't say I didn't warn you." With the information he needed, Reyes thanked Trask and exited the VIP area, returning to where Kresh and McKinley were waiting. Seeing him return, McKinley instantly turned to Reyes, his curious eyes expecting a report.

"So, boss, what's the word?" he asked, his arms crossed as he leaned against the railing.

Reyes nodded, "We know where to find Zaria. She's in District Six, working on a cure for an outbreak."

McKinley whistled, his eyes widening in surprise. "That's the quarantine zone, isn't it? Sounds like a fun trip."

Kresh, standing silent until now, spoke, "A challenge worthy of warriors. We will face it head-on."

"We certainly will," agreed Reyes, with a determined look in his eyes. "Let's get prepared. We're heading to District Six."

With a new lead and a clear mission, the trio left the pulsating club and returned to the streets of Zulu. Every step was a step closer to their next ally, a step closer to their ultimate goal. The fight against Stevens was far from over, but with each passing moment, they were slowly but surely tipping the scales in their favor.

◆ ◆ ◆

Fully equipped the trio stood at the entrance to District Six, a formidable barricade separating it from the rest of Zulu. The air was thick with unease, the buildings beyond the barrier shrouded in darkness.

"All set?" Reyes asked, casting a look at McKinley and Kresh.

"Ready as ever, Commander," McKinley responded, adjusting his

rifle and cracking a grin. "Time for a stroll in the park, yeah?"
Kresh grunted his agreement, his hands flexing around the hilt of his blade. "We walk into the shadows, then. For the mission."
Turning towards the barrier, Reyes gave a nod of approval. He held a sense of trepidation, yet his determination was unwavering. This was for Zaria Nix, for the mission, for the Federation. They would brave whatever lurked in District Six, and they would come out on top.
As they crossed the threshold into the district, the noise of Zulu behind them, they found themselves in an eerily quiet alleyway. The buildings leaned in over them, casting long shadows that stretched across the cracked pavement.
"You sure this is the right way, Commander?" McKinley broke the silence, his voice echoing off the derelict walls. He ran a hand through his hair, glancing around with unease. "Place making me hair stand up."
"According to Trask, she's holed up in the old research facility at the center of the district," Reyes responded, peering at a device in his hand. It was a map of the district, a blinking dot marking their current position. "We just need to keep moving straight."
McKinley made a face but didn't comment, merely tightening his grip on his rifle. Beside him, Kresh remained silent, his intense gaze scanning their surroundings, alert for any movement.
As they ventured deeper into the district, the oppressive silence was replaced by the distant hum of machinery. The derelict buildings gave way to the towering walls of the research facility. It loomed over them, a stark contrast to the dilapidated district around it.
"Looks like we're here," Reyes announced, stopping in front of the enormous structure. He turned to his companions, meeting their gazes with determination. "Remember, our goal is to find Zaria Nix. We're not here to cause a fight, but be ready just in

case."

"Roger that, Commander," McKinley replied, his earlier joviality replaced by focused seriousness. Kresh merely grunted in acknowledgment, his grip on his blade unyielding.

Just as they were about to reach the entrance of the research facility, a group of heavily armed guards stepped out from the shadows. With a firm stance and a stern look, their message was clear - no one was getting past them.

"Halt!" the lead guard called out, raising a hand. "This is a restricted area. Turn around and leave now."

Reyes held up his hands in a sign of peace, stopping in his tracks. "We're here to speak with Dr. Zaria Nix," he said calmly, trying to keep any hint of threat from his voice.

The guard scoffed, "And why would we believe you? You could be here to harm her. Orders are clear: No one enters. No one leaves. If you don't comply, we're authorized to use force."

Reyes glanced at his companions, a silent understanding passing between them. Kresh stood tall and firm, his eyes never leaving the guards, while McKinley shifted his grip on his rifle, ready for whatever was to come.

"Listen, we mean no harm," Reyes insisted, looking back at the guard. "We need to speak with Dr. Nix. It's urgent. It's about Stevens."

The mention of the name caused the guards to falter momentarily, exchanging uncertain glances. Their weapons, however, remained aimed at the trio. The threat was clear: one wrong move, and they would be shot.

The chill of Europa's wind swept across the standoff, and Reyes kept his gaze steady on the guards, one hand resting lightly on the grip of his blaster. "We're here on a mission of mercy," he declared, his voice echoing across the empty street. "We're not here for a fight, but we won't be turned away either."

The guards' expressions hardened, their hands inching towards their own weapons. "You've got no jurisdiction here, Commander. This is our ground," one guard retorted, a note of finality in his voice.

That's when Reyes made his move. With a swift motion, he drew his blaster, the cold metal glinting under the pale light of the moons. "Then it looks like we've got ourselves a disagreement."

Kresh, towering over the rest, responded with a low, rumbling laugh, his scaled hand drawing out his own formidable weapon, its length gleaming ominously in the half-light. "You sure you want to test us, boy?" he challenged, a predatory grin on his face. Next to him, McKinley followed suit, his muscular arm pulling out his own blaster. There was a hard glint in his eyes, a promise of unyielding resolve. "We're not leaving. You'd best stand down," he suggested, the threat implicit in his tone.

The quiet that followed was fraught with tension, each second stretching on as the guards seemed to weigh their options. Reyes' words, hanging in the air, seemed to resonate with a potent mix of promise and threat, turning the previously quiet evening into a powder keg of a situation. The following moments would decide whether this ended peacefully or in a blaze of blaster fire. In the tense silence, the sudden clatter of a door bursting open had everyone turning their heads. Out streamed a group of scientists, lab coats flapping in the wind, looking terribly out of place in the standoff. In the lead was Zaria Nix, her eyes wide with alarm.

"What in the universe are you doing?" Zaria shouted at the guards. She looked to Reyes, eyes narrowing, and back to the guards. "Who gave you the right to draw arms on a Federation officer?"

The leading guard opened his mouth to respond, but Zaria held up her hand, cutting him off. "No, don't bother. I know exactly what you're going to say. Something about territory, jurisdiction, and 'this is our ground'. Right?"

The guard looked taken aback but replied with a bit of bravado, "They're trying to barge their way in here, ma'am, saying something about the galaxy being in trouble and that...that traitor Stevens."

Zaria's eyes widened at the mention of Stevens' name. She turned sharply to Reyes, "Is this true?"

Reyes nodded, keeping his grip firm on his blaster, "Yes, Zaria. We're here to talk to you about that, among other things."

Zaria huffed, pinching the bridge of her nose in annoyance before turning back to the guards. "You imbeciles," she muttered under her breath, loud enough for Reyes to hear. Then louder, "Stand down. That's an order."

"But, ma'am," the guard started to protest.

"I said, stand down," Zaria snapped, her gaze as icy as the Europan wind. "And if I hear that you've drawn your weapons on my visitors again, you'll be answering to me."

The guards reluctantly holstered their weapons, breaking the standoff. Reyes and his companions did the same, their gazes never leaving the guards. Zaria gave them a small, apologetic smile before leading them away from the increasingly bewildered guards. As they moved away from the guards, McKinley grinned at Reyes, his voice filled with amusement, "She's quite a spitfire, isn't she? I like her style."

Reyes chuckled at McKinley's comment, shaking his head at his friend's casual ability to lighten the mood.

Zaria, her anger now subsided, turned to the group with a genuine apology in her eyes, "I'm really sorry about that. They can be... overzealous in their duties."

With a dismissive wave of his hand, Reyes replied, "It happens more often than you'd think. We're getting used to it. Just another day at the office for us, right guys?"

The words were light, but there was a stern edge in Reyes' voice, a veiled warning to the guards. Kresh grunted in agreement, and McKinley's laughter echoed around them, further lightening the mood.

"Now, let's get inside," Zaria said, gesturing to the building behind her, "There's a lot we need to discuss."

As Reyes passed the guards, he shot them a warning glance, a silent promise that he wouldn't forget their little encounter.

The guards could only watch in silence as the trio followed Zaria into the building, the doors closing behind them with a decisive thud.

Once inside, the team was met with an entirely different scene. Instead of the militaristic façade they had encountered outside, the interior of the building was bustling with scientists and researchers, all hard at work. The air was thick with anticipation, the tang of chemicals, and the hum of machinery.

Zaria led them through winding corridors, towards a central control room. Displays of data, complex diagrams, and holographic projections filled the room, casting an ethereal glow. The heart of this operation was undeniably here.

Reyes couldn't help but marvel at the dedication of the people here, the ingenuity of their work. This was a side of Europa that Moore hadn't mentioned.

Yet, he couldn't forget the guards and the isolation they were imposing on these researchers. Something didn't add up.

"You must be wondering about all this," Zaria said, breaking the silence as she indicated the room around them. "This is where we've been developing the cure for the plague that's been ravaging the district. But it's also...more."

Seeing their intrigued faces, Zaria took a deep breath, then revealed, "We were approached by Stevens. He didn't want a cure. He wanted a bioweapon. But we refused."

McKinley whistled lowly, "Guess that's why the district's off-limits, huh?"

Zaria nodded, "The guards, the isolation, it's all Stevens' doing. He was trying to force our hand. But we resisted. And we've been secretly working on the cure ever since."

Reyes could only respect the courage and resolve Zaria and her team had shown. But the revelation of Stevens' involvement sent a chill down his spine. Whatever was happening here, it was bigger and far more dangerous than he had initially thought. And they were right at the center of it. Zaria, her gaze fixed on the numerous displays, looked anxious. There was a gravity to her voice as she finally spoke.

"I can't leave just yet," she began, her voice firm. "Before I can join you, there's something I need to do here. Something important."

Reyes crossed his arms, his brow furrowed. "What do you need?" he asked.

"The final element for the cure," Zaria responded, her fingers dancing across a holographic display. "There's a rare mineral found only deep within Europa's icy crust. It has unique properties that can render the cure stable and viable."

Moore looked over the data displayed. "How deep are we talking?" she questioned.

"Several kilometers," Zaria answered. "There's an old drilling outpost not far from here. It was abandoned years ago when they hit a pocket of geothermal vents. But it's exactly where we need to be."

McKinley cracked a grin, his chest puffing out slightly. "A little spelunkin' mission through ice and steam? Sounds like a day at the beach."

Zaria cast a wary glance at McKinley, then turned to Reyes. "Commander, I know this complicates things. But we have the chance to save lives here, to do some real good. If I'm to leave this place with you, I need to know I've done everything I can."

Reyes' gaze was unwavering as he met Zaria's determined eyes. He was quiet for a moment before he nodded. "Alright, let's get that mineral. But we move fast. McKinley, Kresh, you're with me. Moore, stay here with Dr. M'doius and coordinate with Zaria's team."

McKinley was already checking his equipment, "I knew these thermals would come in handy one day."

As the team began to mobilize, Moore stepped close to Reyes. "Be careful," she whispered.

Reyes offered a slight smile. "When am I not?" he retorted, earning him a roll of Moore's eyes. He then turned to Zaria. "Lead the way."

Together, the group made their way towards the abandoned

drilling outpost, their mission to secure the final element that could bring hope to those affected by the plague and ensure Zaria's valuable cooperation in their battle against Stevens and the growing threat he represented.

CHAPTER 18

The drilling outpost was a weathered behemoth of steel and ice, its monolithic form casting a shadow across the frozen landscape. A sense of desolation hung over the place, the echoes of its past still lingering within the worn, rusty structures. The howling wind and the creaking metal were the only sounds that greeted them.

"Zaria, are we expecting company?" Reyes questioned, his eyes darting around the abandoned complex.

"The outpost was abandoned for a reason, Commander. The geothermal vents made the area too unstable," Zaria replied, her gaze focused on the handheld device scanning the mineral deposits beneath the surface.

Just as she said that, a low rumble echoed through the ground beneath their feet, the shaking causing ice crystals to shower down from the towering outpost. McKinley let out a low whistle.

"You weren't kidding about the instability."

"No," Zaria said, her expression tense. "But we need to hurry."

They moved quickly, descending into the outpost's deep underbelly. Their path lit by the glow of their handheld lights, shadows danced ominously on the ice encrusted walls. As they descended, Zaria's scanner started beeping.

"We're close," she announced. "Just a few more—" Before Zaria could finish her sentence, a sudden, deafening roar echoed through the dimly lit, icy tunnels. A frigid gust of air whipped through the narrow passage, carrying with it the distinctive, acrid stench of the Ice Crawlers. This was a scent known all too well by the inhabitants of Europa – a repugnant mixture of sulfur and rot, indicating the presence of the monstrous creatures. Residing deep within the moon's icy caverns, these beasts were known for their voracious appetite, aggressive nature, and the terror they instilled in the hearts of those unfortunate enough to cross their paths.

Their eyes widened as they turned to face the horde of Ice Crawlers – grotesque and massive, their bodies bore resemblance to a crustacean's exoskeleton, their carapaces glinting in the dim light, teeth gnashing and claws scraping against the frost-covered rock. The very sight of them was enough to freeze the blood in one's veins. Yet there was no time for fear.

"Kresh, McKinley! Hold them off!" Reyes commanded, his voice cutting through the guttural snarls of the incoming beasts. He swiftly unholstered his plasma pistol, its icy blue glow casting an eerie light on his stern face. "Zaria, keep digging. We can't leave without that mineral." Zaria, a dedicated scientist through and through, nodded without hesitation, her hands working with practiced precision as she continued her task. Around her, the tunnel had turned into a battleground. Kresh, with his robust Drakkan physiology, morphed into a whirlwind of raw, scaled fury. He was the embodiment of his warrior race, his four, muscular limbs a blur as he engaged the Ice Crawlers. His heavy, clawed fists sent the creatures skidding across the slick, ice-covered floor, their painful shrieks echoing throughout the cavern. McKinley, on the other hand, was the epitome of a seasoned Federation soldier. His large frame stood firm and unwavering, even as the crawlers descended upon them in droves. His high-powered assault rifle hummed with lethal energy, each pull of the trigger unleashing a blazing torrent of plasma. The air was filled with the distinct smell of ozone as his well-placed shots found their mark, toppling the aggressive Ice Crawlers one by one. McKinley's face was a mask of grim determination, his gaze unflinching as he held the line against the onslaught.

"Reyes, we got more incoming!" McKinley called, his gun spraying a volley of plasma bolts at the oncoming horde.

"Just hold on!" Reyes shouted back, blasting away at the Ice Crawlers, his shots causing the creatures to recoil. In the heat of the battle, Zaria's scanner beeped loudly.

"Got it!" she yelled, extracting a shimmering piece of mineral from the ice. "Let's go!"

With the mineral secured, they fought their way out, escaping the outpost just as a massive geothermal vent erupted, spewing hot steam and forcing the Ice Crawlers back into the depths. Panting and weary, but successful, they watched as the outpost disappeared in their wake.

McKinley let out a breathless laugh. "And here I thought this was just another day at the office."

Despite the adrenaline, Reyes managed a smile. "Never a dull moment, McKinley. Never a dull moment."

With the precious mineral safely secured in Zaria's possession, the urgency of their mission gradually eased. Retracing their steps, they navigated their way through the labyrinthine icy tunnels, leaving the cold, harsh clamor of the Ice Crawlers far behind. Their adrenaline slowly waned, replaced by a collective sigh of relief.

◆ ◆ ◆

Upon their return to the quarantine zone, the imposing gates parted to reveal a scene of organized chaos - scientists hurriedly going about their tasks, the air buzzing with a strange sense of anticipation and hope. The sight of their victorious return, despite the odds they faced, seemed to infuse the atmosphere with a renewed sense of vigor. Zaria, still dusted with icy particles and flushed from the adrenaline, was greeted by a round of applause. Despite her usually reserved nature, a warm, appreciative smile spread across her face. She was one step closer to producing the much-needed cure for the stricken district. Reyes, McKinley, and Kresh watched her, a shared sense of achievement reflecting in their eyes.

"Good work, team," Reyes praised, glancing at his companions, his gaze filled with gratitude and pride. Kresh, the stoic Drakkan warrior, gave a curt nod, his scaly visage incapable of hiding the glimmer of satisfaction in his eyes. McKinley, on the other hand, responded with a wide grin, a twinkle of relief and accomplishment in his gaze. Zaria, this success wasn't just a victory for her research. She was one step closer to joining Reyes' team, a prospect that filled her with a thrilling blend of excitement and trepidation. As she watched the commander interact with his team, her heart swelled with admiration and respect. The dedication, bravery, and unity they exhibited were something she aspired to be a part of. Reyes caught her gaze and gave her a nod of acknowledgment, his eyes shining with unspoken understanding. It was a silent promise - a vow of welcoming her into their ranks, a shared bond of facing the unknown together, a pledge of leaving no one behind. This was just the beginning of their journey together. The cure was within their grasp, and the galaxy's salvation, one step closer to reality. Amidst the flurry of activity, Zaria turned to face Reyes and his team. Her eyes, filled with determination and gratitude, met Reyes' steady gaze. The chatter and bustle around them seemed to dim as she took a deep breath, ready to voice her decision.

"Commander Reyes," she began, her tone resonant over the surrounding noise. "My team and I, we...we can handle it from here. We have the mineral, we have the research, and now, we have the means to produce the cure."

She paused, glancing at the scientists, who were already engrossed in their tasks. Her gaze then returned to the trio. A faint smile graced her lips as she continued, "This is a fight we can handle. But there's a bigger one out there, one that I can no longer ignore. One that I believe I can help with, thanks to you."

McKinley, a playful grin on his face, clapped his hands, "Hear, hear! That's the spirit, doc!"

Kresh grunted his approval, his scales shimmering in the artificial light of the zone. Reyes, his expression serious yet welcoming, extended his hand toward Zaria, "We're glad to have you with us, Zaria."

Zaria took his hand, shaking it firmly. The decision had been made. The path was now clear. She was joining Reyes and his team.

There was a sense of finality to the moment, a promise of the battles to come, and the understanding that they were stepping into the unknown.

As she released his hand, the sounds of the quarantine zone once again rushed in to fill the silence, bringing her back to the reality of her mission here. But now, there was a new layer to her reality - a commitment to a team, a cause, and a commander who had shown her that there was more to the fight than her corner of the galaxy. With a last glance at her team of scientists, she turned, ready to step into this new chapter of her life, a member of Reyes' diverse and dynamic team.

CHAPTER 19

Aboard the Bushido, the crew congregated in the main lounge. The space was filled with comfortable seating and warm, ambient lighting, reflecting off polished metal surfaces and lending the room an inviting glow. As Reyes entered with Zaria at his side, the hum of conversation abruptly ceased. Eyes, both human and alien, turned towards them with curious anticipation.

"Everyone," Reyes began, his deep voice echoing through the room, "I'd like you to meet Dr. Zaria Nix, a renowned scientist from Europa. She's joining us in our mission."

Murmurs of curiosity swept through the room, all eyes now focused on the newcomer. Zaria, caught in the sudden spotlight, offered a small, uncertain wave. "Hi, everyone. Pleasure to be here."

Moore was the first to break the ice. She rose from her seat and approached Zaria with a warm smile, extending her hand. "Dr. Nix, welcome aboard. From what Reyes tells us, you've got quite the knack for getting out of tight spots."

Laughter erupted around the room, easing the tension. The crew introduced themselves, each in their unique way.

Vela, her feathers shimmering under the room's lighting, spoke in her characteristic lyrical tone. "Zaria, we're honored to have you. Your reputation precedes you. The battle at the Ice Crawler nest is a tale for the ages."

Dr. M'doius, her eyes reflecting her keen intellect, greeted Zaria warmly. "Dr. Nix, I've been an admirer of your work for quite some time. I'm looking forward to many stimulating discussions on scientific matters."

Syv, piped in with a hint of humor. "Glad to have another 'brain' on board. Makes my job a tad easier."

Rising from his spot, McKinley crossed the room, his footsteps echoing in the sudden quiet. Stopping in front of Zaria, he extended his hand. "Dr. Nix, welcome to our motley crew. I've got to say, I admire a woman who can stand her ground." A blush rose to Zaria's cheeks, but she accepted the handshake. "Thank you, Sergeant McKinley."

Kresh, the Drakkan brawler, his scales catching the light, grunted in amusement and offered a terse, "Welcome, Dr. Nix."

The rest of the crew continued their introductions, but McKinley's eyes remained on Zaria. Across the room, Moore and Reyes shared a knowing glance, a small smile tugging at their lips. They had another member in their crew, another piece in their fight against the Ascendancy. For now, they could afford a moment of celebration. As the room filled with laughter and conversation, McKinley found himself drawn to Zaria. He was intrigued by her, and he knew he wanted to know her beyond her title as a scientist. The journey ahead was filled with uncertainties, but for now, he relished in the possibility of what could be.

"Commander" Dr. M'doius inquired "What's our next move?" Reyes, catching Dr. M'doius' question, turned his attention back to the gathered crew. The murmur of conversation quieted once again. The room was filled with anticipation and curiosity.

"Now that we've welcomed our newest member, it's time we discuss our next steps," Reyes said, his gaze sweeping across the faces of his team. "Our mission isn't over yet."

Dr. M'doius, her bright eyes glowing with interest, leaned forward slightly. "And what might that be, Commander?" She asked, her melodic voice filling the quiet room. "We have our next target," Reyes said, his eyes briefly flickering towards Moore, who gave a subtle nod of confirmation. "We've been tracking the Ascendancy's activities, and we have a lead. It's brought us to a name Quil Tavash.

"Apologies, Commander Reyes." Syv interrupted. "New data has been received. The situation has changed."

All eyes turned to the Tranakaran pilot, his numerous limbs at work over the control panel, as he projected a new set of data onto the holo-display.

"Quil Tavash is deceased. Terminated in a Federation raid three days ago." The holo-display showed an image of the infamous Zelarian pirate along with the timestamp and location of his demise. "Regrettably, we missed an opportunity."

There was a brief moment of stunned silence before McKinley spoke, "Well, that's a blow to the solar plexus. What's our move now, Reyes?"

Before Reyes could respond, Syv added more. "However, this Federation raid has uncovered significant intelligence. They have located Stevens' base of operations - Mars."

"Mars?" Zaria echoed, her brows furrowing in surprise.

"That's it then." Moore's voice was steady as she met Reyes' gaze. "We need to head to Mars."

Reyes nodded, letting out a breath he didn't realize he was holding. "Looks like the hunt is finally coming to a head. We've got our work cut out for us. Prepare for a full-scale operation."

"And the Federation?" Dr. M'doius questioned, her eyes meeting Reyes'. "What will our relationship be in this confrontation?"

Reyes took a moment, his gaze intense. "I'll get in contact with them, see what they know, but, our priority is stopping Stevens and the Ascendancy."

A wave of determined nods swept across the room. Mars was their next destination. The mission was clearer, the threat ever closer. It was time to brace for the storm.

◆ ◆ ◆

Standing alone in the ships briefing room, Reyes activated the holo-communicator. The holographic figure of Admiral Lawson materialized before him. Tall and stern, with sharp features and a no-nonsense aura, Lawson was known for his strategic mind and hardline tactics. Reyes' eyes narrowed on the holographic figure of Admiral Lawson. He knew a serious conversation was imminent. Lawson's stern gaze fixed on him, his mouth a thin line.

"Commander Reyes," the Admiral began, his voice carrying the gravity of their situation. "You've certainly been keeping yourself busy."

"Admiral Lawson," Reyes responded evenly, squaring his shoulders. "We've been doing what needs to be done."

"Indeed," Lawson nodded, pausing to take a deep breath. "I have been informed of your exploits. Including your impending journey to Mars."

Reyes sat up straight, his eyes never leaving Lawson. "Yes, Admiral. We believe that is where we will find Stevens."

A grim smile twisted Lawson's lips. "We are aware, Commander. Our intel confirms your suspicions. Mars is not just Stevens' hideout; it's his stronghold."

The confirmation sent a chill down Reyes' spine. He hadn't expected Fleet Command to be aware of their movements.

Lawson continued, his gaze as hard as ever. "Fleet Command is mounting a two-fold operation. Our objective is to neutralize Stevens and retake Mars."

Reyes nodded, absorbing the information. He knew what was coming. "What do you need from us, Admiral?"

"We need you, Reyes," Lawson stated matter-of-factly. "You've been leading this charge from the beginning. Your team has the best understanding of what we're up against. You will lead the ground assault."

The enormity of the task ahead filled the room. But Reyes met it head-on, his resolve steeling. "We won't let you down, Admiral."

Lawson gave him a curt nod. "I know you won't, Commander. The Federation is counting on you. Lawson out."

As the holo-communicator blinked off, Reyes found himself staring at the space Lawson's image had occupied. The stakes were high. The fight ahead, tougher than any they had faced before. But with the weight of the Federation on their shoulders, failure was not an option. They would face Stevens and they would win. Mars would be liberated.

◆ ◆ ◆

The team gathered in the Bushido's briefing room, their faces tense with anticipation. Zaria, McKinley, Kresh, Vela, Dr. M'doius, Syv, and Moore settled into their seats, looking expectantly at Reyes who was standing in front of the holo-display.
Reyes cleared his throat and looked over the assembled team. His gaze was stern but carried a hint of pride. He flicked a switch, and a holographic image of Mars appeared, rotating slowly in the air.
"We're going to Mars," he announced, his voice steady.
A murmur rippled through the room.
"Mars? What's on Mars?" Zaria inquired, her eyebrows knitting together.
"That's where Stevens has set up his base. Moreover, he has turned the Martian Republic to his side. The Federation is mounting an operation to take him down and liberate Mars. We," Reyes said, pointing at each member of the crew, "will lead the ground assault."
Dr. M'doius raised an eyebrow. "What can we expect from the enemy?"
"Heavy resistance," Reyes said gravely. "Stevens has amassed considerable forces, and the Martian Republic's technology is advanced."
Kresh pounded his chest with a fist. "We are ready for battle. I was born in the fires of war."
Vela's feathered crest stood on end, her talons gripping the armrest. "We stand with you, Commander."
Moore's voice, always composed, held an edge of steel. "We all knew this was coming. We're ready."

Reyes looked at each face before him – warriors, scholars, survivors. His family. His voice grew louder, his words echoing through the room.

"We stand on the edge of a precipice. Before us lies a tempest, the storm of war. Our enemies have sown the winds of tyranny, of corruption, of despair. And I say unto you," Reyes' voice boomed, "those who sow the wind, will reap the whirlwind!"

The crew leaned forward, their eyes fixed on Reyes.

"We are that whirlwind! We are the tempest that will sweep across Mars and tear down the citadel of our enemies!

We carry the hopes, the dreams, and the futures of countless souls in our hands. We stand united, a family born of courage and bound by a purpose!"

He moved around the table, looking at each one of them. His voice dropped to a growl, "We will face horrors. We will face a foe that believes itself invincible. But let it be known that today, in this room, stands an assembly of invincible spirits. We are the protectors, the sword and the shield! We are the beacon in the night!"

As he finished, he placed his hand on the holographic image of Mars.

The room was silent for a heartbeat and then erupted into cheers and shouts. The crew stood, clapping each other on the shoulders, their eyes gleaming with resolve. Reyes gave a final nod, his heart swelling with pride for the crew that had become more than just comrades – they were his brothers and sisters in arms. They were the whirlwind. And they would sweep across Mars with all the fury and might that they could muster. As the applause and cheers began to die down, McKinley, who had been grinning widely throughout the speech, stood up and raised his hand for silence.

"Whirlwind, huh?" McKinley said, his voice carrying through the room, and his eyes twinkling. "That would make for a mighty crew name, Commander."

Reyes turned toward McKinley and let a slow grin spread across his face. "I have one better," he replied, his voice brimming with newfound enthusiasm.

The room grew quiet as everyone leaned in, curious to hear what Reyes had to say.

"Operation Whirlwind," he declared.

The crew erupted into applause and cheers once again, clapping McKinley on the back, and offering words of approval.

Zaria, who was standing next to McKinley, chimed in, "It's perfect. A storm they'll never forget!"

Dr. M'doius, usually composed and reserved, offered a rare smile. "A most apt title, Commander. The Erisian archives speak of the power of names and words. They have weight and resonate through the stars."

Moore stood up and looked at Reyes with admiration in her eyes. "Operation Whirlwind it is. We'll make sure that the name will be remembered for ages."

Reyes nodded. "Then let's get ready. We have a storm to unleash upon our enemies."

As the crew began dispersing to prepare for the mission, McKinley sidled up next to Reyes.

"You know, Commander, I've been through a lot, but that speech of yours..." McKinley's voice cracked a bit. "It's an honor to be a part of this."

Reyes placed a hand on McKinley's shoulder. "The honor is mine, Sergeant. We're all in this together. We are Operation Whirlwind."

Together, they turned and made their way to the command deck, ready to take on the storm that awaited them on Mars.

CHAPTER 20

As the Bushido approached Mars, the crew gazed out the viewscreens at the massive fleet that had assembled. Various Federation warships, frigates, and cruisers dotted the black canvas of space, all aligned for a singular purpose. One ship stood out among the rest, the FSS Independence. Its sleek, yet formidable structure was reminiscent of a sword ready to cut through the void. Reyes couldn't help but feel a surge of emotion as he recognized the ship that had saved them when the FSS Undaunting fell. Suddenly, the communications channel beeped, and a familiar face appeared on the screen. It was Captain Claudia Avery of the FSS Independence.

"Commander Reyes," Captain Avery greeted with a grin, "I never thought we'd be meeting like this again, especially with you commanding that impressive ship of yours."

Reyes responded with a smile. "Captain Avery, it's good to see you. The FSS Independence is looking as formidable as ever."

"Thank you, Commander," Captain Avery replied. "And might I say, the Bushido is quite the ship. A far cry from that rock I picked you off of."

Moore, who was standing next to Reyes, chuckled. "We've come a long way since then."

"We certainly have," Captain Avery agreed. "I'm just sorry it's under these circumstances."

"There's no one I'd rather have at my side in a battle than you and the crew of the Independence," Reyes said earnestly.

"Likewise," Captain Avery responded, her tone turning serious. "This mission… it's not going to be easy."

"We know," said Reyes. "But we can't let Stevens and his forces go unchecked."

"You're right," Captain Avery nodded. "We'll be right beside you, every step of the way."

Reyes gave a nod of gratitude. "Thank you, Captain."

As the channel closed, McKinley looked over at Reyes. "She seems like a good one to have in our corner."

Reyes agreed, "Definitely. Now, let's get ready. Operation Whirlwind begins now."

The Bushido took its place among the fleet as they prepared to make their descent to Mars, with the determination to end Stevens' reign and bring peace to the galaxy.

◆ ◆ ◆

On the bridge, the crew was tense as two gargantuan Federation warships, the FSS Titan and FSS Goliath, took their positions in the orbit of Mars. The colossal cannons on these warships fired barrages of plasma projectiles, lighting up the Martian atmosphere with a torrential downpour of destruction. From the Bushido, the impacts on the Martian surface were visible as flashes of bright light, marking the beginning of the battle.

"This is it," whispered Moore as she secured her restraints.

"The big leagues," McKinley added, his face stern as he gripped his blaster rifle.

As the Bushido started its descent, Syv's nimble fingers danced across the controls while his multi-faceted eyes scanned multiple readouts simultaneously.

"Taking evasive maneuvers," Syv announced as the ship zigzagged through space, narrowly dodging enemy laser batteries and cannon fire.

"We're under heavy fire!" Dr. M'doius warned, her eyes wide. "Shields at 76%!"

Zaria Nix, at the engineering console, chimed in, "I'm rerouting power to the shields. Hang on!"

Reyes stood in the center of the bridge, gripping the back of Syv's chair. "Take us down as close to the target coordinates as you can, Syv."

"Affirmative, Commander. But, we are coming in at high velocity. I recommend everyone secure themselves," Syv's robotic voice conveyed the urgency.

The crew braced themselves as the ship shook violently. McKinley turned to Zaria, shouting over the cacophony, "First time in a combat drop?"

Zaria shouted back, "I'm more used to labs than lasers, but I'm not backing down!"

Outside the ship, the Martian surface loomed closer and closer as the ship continued its rapid descent.

"Brace for impact!" Syv shouted.

With a thunderous crash, the Bushido landed, skidding across the rocky terrain.

Kresh, who had been silent until now, unsheathed his massive Drakkan blade. "For honor and the galaxy!" he roared.

"Hooah!" echoed McKinley.

Reyes gathered himself and turned to face his crew. His voice was calm but firm, "We've trained for this. We fight not just for ourselves, but for all the innocent lives that are in the balance. We are the last line of defense. Remember, those who sow the wind, will reap the whirlwind."

The crew's faces hardened with resolve as they nodded.

"Moore, Kresh, McKinley, Zaria, Dr. M'doius, take the east flank. I'll head straight for Stevens."

They all moved with purpose as the hatch opened, revealing the chaotic Martian battlefield.

As the team disembarked, the roar of weapons fire and the clash of metal on metal enveloped them. The Battle for Mars had begun. Blaster fire and explosions rocked the Martian landscape. The ground forces of the Federation were engaging in fierce combat with the Martian Republic forces and mercenaries loyal to Stevens. Reyes surveyed the chaos around him and was preparing to head straight for Stevens when a booming voice hollered over the cacophony of battle.

"Commander! Hold!" Kresh roared, his hulking Drakkan frame making its way through the troops towards Reyes.

"What is it, Kresh?" Reyes shouted back, as blaster bolts zipped past them.

Kresh's scaly face came close to Reyes, his voice heavy with determination. "I'm coming with you. We Drakkans do not back down from a worthy adversary, and Stevens has made it personal. You owe me that much," he thundered, the blade in his hand gleaming.

Reyes looked at Kresh, his eyes intense and unwavering. He then broke into a grim smile. "Alright, Kresh, let's take that bastard down together."

As they made their way through the battlefield, they saw Federation troops pushing back the mercenaries and Mars Republic forces. McKinley and Zaria were laying down covering fire for the advancing troops, while Dr. M'doius attended to wounded soldiers.

Moore, noticing Reyes and Kresh breaking off, shouted, "Commander, take this!" She tossed him a small device. "It's a portable shield generator. It might buy you some time!"

Reyes caught it and nodded his thanks. Kresh and Reyes moved with relentless determination. Kresh's Drakkan strength cleared a path through the enemies, while Reyes' sharpshooting picked off targets with deadly accuracy. They were within the threshold of the compound when Reyes' comms crackled to life. It was McKinley, his voice strained and frantic.

"Commander! You need to hear this!" McKinley yelled through the comms.

Reyes ducked behind a pillar as Kresh covered him, blaster bolts ricocheting everywhere. "Report, McKinley!" Reyes shouted back.

"I stumbled upon something, some kind of weapon," McKinley replied breathlessly. "Stevens' goons are all over this place, and it seems like they're in a rush to set it off. I don't think I can hold them much longer!"

Before Reyes could reply, Moore's voice cut through the comms. "Reyes! We're pinned down by a laser battery. They've got us surrounded. I don't know how long we can hold out!"

Reyes' heart pounded in his chest. His mind raced as he processed the information. He had a decision to make - to save McKinley or Moore.

Kresh yelled over the blaster fire, "Commander, make your choice! But remember, we are here to stop Stevens and whatever madness he's planning!"

Reyes looked up, his gaze sharp and fierce. He opened the comms.

"McKinley, listen to me," Reyes spoke with a stern resolve, "You've been my right hand since day one. I need you to do whatever you can to sabotage that weapon. The entire galaxy is depending on it."

"I understand, Commander," McKinley's voice was somber yet resolute. "It's been an honor."

"No, the honor was mine," Reyes said, his voice breaking for a moment. He then switched channels. "Moore, we're coming for you. Hang tight!"

As Reyes and Kresh fought their way through the compound, their path towards Moore was a blur of chaos and adrenaline. A cacophony of blaster fire, screams, and metallic clangs surrounded them. The ground suddenly quaked violently, and a shockwave rippled through the air. Reyes was thrown off balance, but Kresh, with his immense Drakkan strength, kept him upright.

"What was that?!" Kresh roared over the din.

Reyes' eyes widened as he saw an intense, blinding light illuminate the horizon. The light was accompanied by a thunderous roar that shook the very core of Mars.

"McKinley..." Reyes whispered, realizing that his comrade had detonated the weapon in an attempt to prevent it from falling into the wrong hands.

They didn't have time to grieve. A new resolve, a furious energy, fueled their movements as they pushed on. As they advanced, Kresh's warrior instincts kicked into overdrive. He tore through Stevens' soldiers like a hurricane through a field. With each swing of his arms, enemies were thrown aside like ragdolls. Reyes moved with a grace and ferocity that could only be described as otherworldly. His blaster seemed to be an extension of himself, each shot finding its mark, as he covered Kresh and ensured no one could flank them.

"Commander, on your left!" Kresh bellowed.

Reyes pivoted and unleashed a hail of blaster fire at a turret that had powered up and taken aim at them. The two warriors continued their relentless assault, their synergy becoming something of legend in that moment. They cut through enemy lines until they finally reached Moore's position. They found Moore and her team pinned down near a massive laser battery that was causing havoc for the allied forces.

"Kresh, take that battery down!" Reyes ordered.

Kresh grinned, his reptilian eyes gleaming with savage delight. He lunged at the laser battery, tearing through the metal and ripping out cables with his bare hands.

Reyes, meanwhile, laid down covering fire as Moore and her team regrouped.

With a final, primal roar, Kresh tore the laser battery apart, and it exploded in a burst of light and smoke.

They had made it. They had saved Moore and her team, but the battle was far from over. They needed to regroup and face Stevens.

Reyes' gaze fell upon the distant horizon once more, where the light from the weapon's detonation still lingered. He swore to himself that McKinley's sacrifice would not be in vain. She nodded, tears welling in her eyes, but her resolve unwavering. They reassembled what was left of their team and headed back to the compound to confront Stevens, knowing that they had to honor McKinley's sacrifice by stopping the evil that threatened the galaxy once and for all.

Reyes and Kresh moved forward beyond them a massive inner sanctum, Moore and the others took point at various exits to protect their flanks.

"We will guard the exits Commander." Moore said proudly "Go get that bastard."

As Reyes and Kresh stormed into the inner sanctum, they were met with an eerie silence that was almost as unnerving as the chaos outside. Before them was a massive chamber, illuminated by a pulsating, unearthly glow. At the far end stood Stevens, perched on a raised platform, his gaze fixed upon them.

His appearance was grotesque. His skin was stretched thin, his eyes glowed with an alien energy, and an aura of madness and power surrounded him.

"You made it, Commander Reyes," Stevens spoke, his voice now haunting and resonant. "Though perhaps not in the way you had planned."

"What... what have you become? What is this madness?" Reyes called out.

"A herald," Stevens replied, his voice echoing through the chamber. "A harbinger of a new dawn."

He gestured to his sides where Reyes and Kresh saw that a group of guards flanked him. They were as grotesque as Stevens, transformed into something beyond human.

"See, Reyes, my discovery here, on Mars, was just the beginning. The obelisks, the signals you received... they were a message, a beckoning from beyond."

Suddenly, behind Stevens, a swirling vortex of light and energy appeared. It was a portal, flickering and unstable, but within, Reyes could see flashes of an alien landscape and bizarre, indescribable creatures.

"I've spent years perfecting this, and now we are on the verge of bridging our world with theirs," Stevens continued. "Imagine the possibilities."

Reyes' heart raced. This was what he had seen in his vision. This was what the obelisks had warned him about.

"You're playing with forces you don't understand, Stevens! This isn't a bridge, it's an invasion!" Reyes shouted, gripping his weapon.

"The sacrifices are necessary. Humanity has to evolve, and through me, it will," Stevens declared.

Kresh growled beside Reyes. "Commander, we need to destroy that portal!"

Stevens pressed a button and the portal flickered more aggressively, revealing more of the other side. Monstrous beings loomed within, eyes focused on Reyes.

Reyes looked at Kresh. "Cover me!"

Kresh launched himself at Stevens' guards with ferocity while Reyes aimed at the machinery powering the portal.

"You could have been part of this, Reyes!" Stevens bellowed as the chamber filled with blaster fire and the roars of Kresh.

Reyes's focus sharpened; he remembered McKinley's sacrifice, the team that relied on him, and the countless lives at stake.

As the chamber filled with blaster fire and the ferocious roar of Kresh battling Stevens' guards, Reyes aimed at the machinery powering the portal. His heart raced, and his focus was unyielding.

Stevens, realizing what Reyes was doing, lunged toward him, his eyes blazing with unnatural light. Kresh, seeing Stevens' intention, threw one last guard against the wall and turned to intercept him.

But Reyes was quicker. He sidestepped Stevens' lunge and with a swift, determined motion, drove his blade into Stevens' chest.

Stevens coughed, his eyes widening. The portal behind them flickered wildly as the machinery began to fail.

"You fool..." Stevens gasped, blood trickling down his chin. "The Ascendency... cannot be stopped. You're only... slowing... the inevitable. They will find a way... and when they do... freedom."

His voice trailed off as the light in his eyes faded. Stevens went limp, and Reyes withdrew his blade.

The portal was now convulsing with raw, unbridled energy. The alien beings on the other side were barely visible through the maelstrom.

"Reyes, we need to go now!" Kresh shouted, grabbing his shoulder.

As they turned to leave, Reyes shot one final glance at the dead Stevens. This was the man who had set so much in motion, who had nearly unleashed an unimaginable horror upon the galaxy.

Reyes and Kresh raced out of the chamber as the portal imploded with a deafening roar, sending shockwaves through the facility.

Rubble and debris flew everywhere as the two of them barely made it out of the collapsing structure.

Once outside, they were greeted by the rest of their team - Moore, Zaria, Dr. M'doius, and Syv. Their faces were a mixture of relief and exhaustion.

Reyes looked up at the Martian sky, still tinged with the light of the battle above, and whispered a silent thanks to those who had given everything for this victory.

As they gathered around him, he could feel the weight of what they had accomplished. They had faced the unknown and stood strong.

"The Ascendency will come again," Reyes said solemnly to his team. "And when they do, we will be waiting. For McKinley and all the others, we will never stop fighting."

They had sown the wind, and in their courage and sacrifice, they had reaped the whirlwind. The galaxy was safe, for now.

CHAPTER 21

The sun was setting behind the grand spires of the memorial hall on Earth. A somber mood prevailed as the air was filled with the scent of freshly cut grass and flowers. People had gathered in uniforms, both military and civilian, to honor a hero who had fallen. In front of a large display showing a picture of McKinley in his Federation uniform, his easy smile captured in time, there lay a coffin draped with the Federation's flag. The light filtering through the stained glass windows cast a golden hue upon it. Reyes, in his full dress uniform, stood at the head of the line with his team behind him. The clasp of his Federation wings was in his hand, and his face was a mask of quiet resolve and sadness. Kresh, who stood much taller than the others, was wearing a Drakkan ceremonial armor. His large clawed hands gently holding his Federation badge. His usually fierce eyes were softened, his broad snout turned down in a rare show of grief.

Moore, elegant and stoic in her uniform, had her lips pressed together, holding back the emotions that threatened to overflow.

Zaria Nix, who had only known McKinley for a short time, wore an expression of respectful mourning. Her scientist uniform bore a single Federation insignia in honor of McKinley.

Dr. M'doius and Syv, in their respective uniforms, completed the line.

One by one, they stepped forward.

Reyes was the first. He placed his Federation wings on McKinley's coffin with a soft click. He then stood upright, saluted sharply, and as tears welled in his eyes, whispered, "Fly high, my friend."

Kresh was next. His massive form was almost tender as he placed his badge next to Reyes'. He raised his clawed hand in a Drakkan salute. His voice, usually booming, was a low rumble. "In the stars, we find peace."

Moore's steps were measured. Her badge joined the others, and her salute was unwavering. She said nothing, but her eyes spoke volumes.

Zaria's movements were graceful. She placed her badge, saluted, and whispered, "Thank you."

Dr. M'doius and Syv followed suit, with gestures of respect that spanned cultures and species.

As they turned and began to leave the hall, the sunset bathed them in a warm, golden light. They did not speak, for no words were needed. They had each other, and in that moment, bound by honor and sacrifice, they were not just a team but a family. In the silence, the echo of McKinley's laughter seemed to surround them. His spirit was still there, among the stars, flying high and free. As Reyes and the team were making their way out of the memorial hall, a figure in a pristine Admiral's uniform was standing to the side, waiting. It was Admiral Lawson, his grizzled features and stern expression softened by the occasion.

"Commander Reyes," Lawson greeted as he extended a hand.

Reyes took it firmly. "Admiral Lawson."

"My deepest condolences for your loss. McKinley was an exemplary soldier and a true Brit through and through," Lawson's voice held a hint of personal sorrow. "I had the honor of serving alongside him once. A spirited character he was."

Reyes managed a small smile. "He never backed down from anything. His spirit was contagious."

"Indeed," Lawson nodded. "How are the rest holding up?"

"They're managing. We all knew what we signed up for, but it doesn't make it any easier," Reyes admitted.

Lawson's gaze turned contemplative as he looked at the team who were speaking quietly amongst themselves. "Commander, I have a proposition for you."

Reyes raised an eyebrow. "I'm listening."

Lawson cleared his throat. "The Federation is in need of strong leaders. Men and women who have seen the face of the unknown and stood their ground. After your actions on Mars and your unyielding dedication to the Federation... How does Admiral Reyes sound to you?"

Reyes blinked in surprise. The weight of the proposition hung heavily in the air.

"You'd have resources at your disposal, the ability to make real change," Lawson continued.

Reyes glanced back at the coffin, then turned to his crew. His family. He saw Kresh talking animatedly with Zaria, Moore sharing a memory of McKinley with Dr. M'doius, and Syv, as ever, watching over them.

He then looked at the Admiral. "Admirals don't fly, do they?" Reyes inquired.

Lawson shook his head. "No, they usually don't."

Reyes took a deep breath and then smiled as he made his decision. "I'm sorry, Admiral Lawson. But I think I'm happy just where I belong. With my family, among the stars. That's where McKinley would want me to be."

Lawson looked at him for a long moment and then broke into a smile. "I had a feeling you'd say that. But I had to try. Take care, Commander. The Federation is better for having you." They shook hands once more.

As Reyes turned to leave, Lawson called out, "Oh, and Reyes?"

Reyes turned back.

"Give 'em hell out there, for McKinley," Lawson said with a nod.

Reyes gave a sharp salute and with a final, "Always," he walked back to his crew.

As they left the memorial hall, the team surrounding him, Reyes couldn't help but feel McKinley's spirit with them, urging them on to their next adventure among the stars.

❖ ❖ ❖

The interior of the Bushido was buzzing with activity as the team prepared for their new mission. The hum of the engines and the clatter of equipment created a familiar backdrop as Reyes stood in the bridge, reviewing the mission details on a holo-display.
Moore entered the bridge, holding a data pad. "Reyes, are you sure about these coordinates? They're quite far out," she said.
"That's what the Federation sent us," he replied, his brow furrowed.
Kresh joined them, his towering form leaning in to study the data. "Slavers this far out? It doesn't make sense," he grumbled.
"Exactly," Reyes muttered. "But orders are orders."
Zaria came jogging onto the bridge, "Reyes, I've been running some scans on the location. I'm picking up something weird."
"Weird how?" Moore asked.
"Like there's more than just slavers out there," Zaria said, her eyes wide. "Much more."
Dr. M'doius joined them, his medical equipment clinking in his pockets. "Is it the Ascendency?" he asked in his deep voice.
"I can't tell. But it's big," Zaria replied.
Syv, who was at the navigation console, suddenly spoke. "Commander, we are receiving an encrypted transmission."
"Put it through," Reyes ordered.
The holo-display flickered and showed a figure cloaked in shadows. The voice was distorted. "Commander Reyes. The Federation doesn't want you close to what really matters. The Ascendency is real and your efforts against them haven't gone unnoticed. Be vigilant."
The transmission ended abruptly.
"What the hell was that?" Moore exclaimed.
Reyes' heart raced. He turned to the crew, his expression intense. "Syv, change course. We need to investigate the original coordinates."

"But the mission…" Zaria started.

"This is bigger than some slavers. I have a feeling we're on the edge of something enormous. If the Ascendency is out there, then we are the first line of defense," Reyes spoke with determination.

"Are we going rogue?" Kresh grinned.

"No," Reyes replied, his gaze steel. "We're doing what's right. For McKinley, for the Federation, and for the galaxy."

The crew's determination ignited, mirroring his. As the Bushido veered off course, racing towards the unknown, Reyes couldn't help but wonder what they were about to uncover. The mysterious transmission, the Ascendency, the bizarre coordinates — it all pointed to a bigger picture they had only begun to uncover. As the stars streaked past the windows, Reyes made a silent vow that they would face whatever was coming head-on, as a family, as a crew. The Bushido charged forward, towards the unknown, as the shadows of a much larger conflict loomed over them.

ABOUT THE AUTHOR

Johnathan Greene

Johnathan is a North Carolina native, author of the books, "Galaxy at Dawn" and "Dangerous Dark." They love all things dealing with space!

Made in United States
Orlando, FL
26 June 2023